# CARMELO'S WAY: 187 ASSASSINS

## A.G. Deberry

# Carmelo's Way: 187 Assassins

Copyright © 2021 by  A.G. Deberry

All rights reserved.
Author: A.G. Deberry
Publisher: Deberry Publishing, LLC
ISBN No: 978-1-6671-1975-5
Editing: Johanna Petronella Leigh
Typesetting: Ricacabrex
Graphic Designer: Ricacabrex
Contact Information: dbpublishing776@gmail.com

# Chapter 1

# Carmelo

At the age of sixteen, Carmelo Graham stood five foot ten and weighed one hundred fifty-five pounds. He had a hairless face, mini afro, and a boyish smile. A person would look at him and think he was the nicest boy in the world. He was polite and respectful to adults, charming to females, and if you didn't know him, you would want him to be your son's best friend or future son-in-law, and for some, even their son.

To the streets, he was known as Menace. A name given to him by his childhood friends. Carmelo stayed in a Blood neighborhood, and although a lot of his friends were Bloods, he chose to remain neutral. The name Menace came after the fights he got into for being affiliated with the Bloods and the murder he committed after one of his childhood friends was killed.

Carmelo sat on the porch overlooking the highway and contemplated his situation. It had been six months since he committed his first murder, and instead of things changing and moving forward, he felt like he'd taken four steps back. His reputation had grown, and the respect was nice, but looking over his shoulder everywhere he went wasn't pleasant at all. Neither was the police arresting him for PC murder over the weekend or finding out he had three females pregnant.

As he took a pull off the blunt, Carmelo shook his head. He didn't have any money to help raise his kids or hire a lawyer if the police ever found enough evidence to charge him. His friends were very quick to give him a gun, but nobody threw him a dope sack to sell. The more he thought about it, the angrier he became. Instead, Carmelo began watching cars drive by in the rain, and enjoyed his blunt.

# Chapter 2

# Brian

Brian a.k.a. B-Dog, sat in his truck and replayed the conversation he had with his cousin, Tanya. She stood five foot four with hazel eyes, brown skin, full lips, and long black hair. She had a beautiful face and a sexy body. If a nigga didn't have money, she wouldn't even acknowledge his existence.

The nigga she was fucking with was a brick man from Detroit named Lil Jay. Tanya was used to getting pampered. Men paid her rent, bought her cars, and took her on shopping sprees. However, Lil Jay was used to having bad bitches and treated Tanya like she was ordinary. She thought the reason she wasn't getting any money was because she wasn't giving him any pussy, so she fucked him. When that didn't work, she got mad.

"Brian, not only was I nice to this nigga, playing the model bitch, I let the nigga hit the pussy. This pussy!" she said, using both hands to point between her legs.

Brian couldn't help but laugh.

"It's not funny, Brian. I'm mad as fuck. Not only did this nigga try to treat me like a nothing ass bitch, but the nigga also has a little dick! He couldn't even make me cum. I'm not lying, B. Got me oohing and aahing like he's King Kong or somebody, ol' chimp dick ass nigga."

"Yo, T?" Brian smiled and held his hands up. "Tanya, focus. Get back to the money."

Tanya sat down. "Brian, I'm not lying, the nigga's got thousands. I've seen two or three different shoe boxes stacked with money."

"What about dope? Guns?"

"He keeps a couple of guns in the house, but I've never seen dope."

Brian was quiet for a while, then he looked at Tanya. "Tell me about the layout . . ."

The more Brian thought about it, the more he knew he couldn't do this on his own. It was too risky.

At twenty-five, Brian was considered an O.G. He'd been in the Blood neighborhood his entire life and been a Blood since the age of ten. Fifteen years later, Brian didn't trust his homies like he did growing up.

In high school, he met a Native American female named Melinda. The two of them fell in love, had two kids, Brian and Brianna, and eventually married. What Brian didn't know was Melinda was going to receive seventy-five thousand a month from her tribe when she turned eighteen years old.

When Brian began driving through the hood in nice cars on 15-inch gold and chrome Daytons, his homies seemed happy for him, but when Melinda's sister, Maria, turned eighteen two years later, their feelings changed. Maria wasn't interested in any of them, and they blamed him for Maria's rejections. Brian spent most of his time with the Y.G. homies and knew that none of them were ready for the job he was about to do. As he pulled out of Tanya's driveway, one thing was for certain. If he didn't find somebody he could trust soon, he wasn't going to do it . . . no matter how Tanya felt.

# Chapter 3

---

# Carmelo

"Fuck you, nigga."

"Nah, fuck with me."

"You walk around here like you run this fuckin' house or something. You don't run shit."

"I see you hung up the phone."

Carmelo opened his eyes and looked outside. He didn't know how long he'd slept, but the rain had stopped. He heard his siblings arguing and took a deep breath. Sometimes he hated living there. Cathy, his siblings' mom, lived in a five-bedroom house overlooking the highway. With her six kids, a grandson, granddaughter, Carmelo, and their younger brother Carl living in such tight corridors, there was never a dull moment. Right now, Carmelo's older brother Chermaine, a.k.a. C.J., was arguing with their sister Chirese. Carmelo stood, stretched, and grabbed his Glock .9 from between the sofa cushions.

He put the pistol on his waist and walked into the house. His sisters Carmen and Carla sat on the couch with Chirese, staring at C.J., who was sitting in the dining room talking on the phone. C.J.

had been out of prison for two years and assumed he was the man of the house since their dad didn't live there.

Carmelo ignored them and walked into the kitchen. His brothers Chris and Carl sat at the table listening to Warren G's "Regulator."

"Where you been at, nigga?" Chris asked.

"I was on the porch."

"What were you doing out there?"

"Shit."

"You were just sitting out there?"

"Nah, nigga, I fell asleep. Why?" Carmelo asked, irritated.

"Bunny and Crystal have been calling looking for you. Where's your pager?"

"Why?"

"'Cause they said you weren't answering it."

"I turned it off." Carmelo reached down and turned his pager back on.

"Oh, okay. What are you about to get into?"

Carl reached over and turned the radio up. Carmelo stared at Carl, then walked over to the radio and turned it off.

"What you do that for?" Carl asked.

"Nigga, you saw us talking."

"So. Y'all weren't talking to me."

"So the fuck what. That doesn't mean turn the shit up."

"You ain't gotta be yelling at me either, nigga. You ain't my daddy."

"Quit doing dumb shit then," Carmelo said and turned his attention back to Chris. "What were you saying now, nigga?"

"What are you about to get into?" Chris asked again.

"Shit. About to grab me something to eat and then probably go to Bunny's pad for the night. Too much shit is going on around here for me right now."

Carmelo opened the refrigerator and closed it. "Damn! Ain't shit to eat. All these muthafuckas staying here and we ain't got no food in the house."

"Nigga, you ain't put no food in the house," C.J. said as he walked into the kitchen.

"Nigga, neither did you," Carmelo replied.

"Start putting some food in the house before you start complaining about no food being in the house."

Carmelo looked at his brother. "Nigga, you start putting some food in the house before you start opening your mouth talking shit."

Carmelo's three sisters walked into the kitchen and stood behind him.

"Yeah, nigga, running around like you're big and bad but ain't doing shit but running your mouth," Chirese said over Carmelo's shoulder.

"Shut up, bitch. Ain't nobody talking to you," C.J. retorted to Chirese.

"You're the bitch, nigga!" Chirese said.

"Fuck you, you soft ass nigga!" Carla yelled.

"Bitch ass nigga!" Carmen said.

C.J. pulled up his pants and started walking toward the girls. When they saw him coming, they began to back up.

"Keep talking and I'ma fuck one of y'all up."

The closer C.J. walked towards the girls the quieter they became. He stopped in front of Carmelo.

"What's up? You got a problem with me?"

"If I did, I'd tell you," Carmelo said, looking C.J. up and down.

"'Cause I'll beat your lil' ass too."

"You'll be dead if you try," Carmelo told C.J.

"What did you say?" C.J. asked in an intimidating tone.

"Nigga, you heard me."

Carmelo and C.J. stared at each other for what seemed like an eternity.

"I'm out of here," Carmelo said and turned to walk out the kitchen.

C.J. took a few steps toward him. "Nigga we ain't done."

Without turning around or missing a step, Carmelo lifted his shirt so that the butt of the Glock was showing.

"Yes, we are," he said as he walked out the door.

# Chapter 4

---

# Brian

Brian drove down 35th and Stevens Avenue with a lot on his mind. *It's a good lick*, he thought. *Two or three shoeboxes of money, and no telling what else.*

He didn't have to jack niggas, his wife was rich by hood definition, so he was straight. Brian craved the excitement and felt as if he was pulling his weight when he did. He was approaching the middle of the block when he saw Menace a couple of houses ahead. He was happy to see the lil' nigga and quickly swerved to the curve without thinking. Brian saw Menace pull his gun out in one swift motion and stopped his truck.

He put his hands in the air shielding his face, hoping the lil nigga wouldn't shoot. He was relieved when he saw Menace look in the truck and lower his gun.

"What the fuck, nigga? You know not to be swerving and jumping on curbs. I almost shot you. You lucky I know how your ride looks," Carmelo told Brian.

"My fault, lil' nigga," Brian apologized as Carmelo put the gun on his waist.

"What's up?" Carmelo asked.

"Shit. What are you about to get into?"

"Nothing. Just got into it with my brother. I had to get out of the house before I caught a case."

"Get in the truck and ride with me."

Carmelo got in and Brian pulled off.

"Why are you so quiet?" Brian asked after a while.

"I got a lot on my mind."

"How old are you?"

"I'll be seventeen in two weeks."

"So, what's on your mind?"

Brian waited as Carmelo looked straight ahead. After a while, he opened his mouth and told Brian everything. He talked about having three females pregnant, the crowded house, and having no money for anything. The more he talked, the more Brian felt he had the right person.

"Can I trust you?" Brian asked when Carmelo finished his story.

"Huh?" Carmelo looked at him confused.

"Can I trust you?"

"Yeah, you can trust me," Carmelo said with confidence.

"I'm going to give you one chance," Brian told him. "And if you fuck up or fuck me over, I'm cutting you off. You understand?"

"Yeah, I understand."

Brian pulled into the parking lot of Portland Foods. "You hungry, nigga?"

"Starving."

"Come on. Let's go in here and get something to eat."

# Chapter 5

# B-Dog

"Remember, do not hit her. Tie her up, talk shit to her, threaten her, but do not hit or hurt her. She's with us. Got it?" Brian told Carmelo.

"Got it."

"Come on, she left the back door open."

Brian opened the screen door slowly, trying to make as little noise as possible. He turned the knob and pushed, expecting it to open. When it didn't, he looked at Carmelo puzzled and tried again. As he reached for the door handle, they heard the door being unlocked. Carmelo pointed his Glock at the door as it quickly opened, causing Brian to stumble into the house.

Tanya wore a white lace bra and thong panty set. She looked at Brian and shook her head.

"Damn, nigga," Tanya whispered. "Keep the noise down."

"If the door would have been unlocked like it was supposed to, this shit wouldn't have happened," Brian whispered back.

"Who is this?" Tanya asked when she saw Carmelo.

"Don't worry about him. Let's get this shit over with."

"Give me five minutes to get back into bed and then come up. His gun is on the dresser by the bed," Tanya told them and headed up the stairs.

"You ready?" Brian asked.

Carmelo put the bandana around his face. "Let's go."

"I'll handle him, you handle her. Handcuff her and I'll do the rest," Brian told Carmelo when they reached the top of the stairs.

They entered the room and saw Lil Jay sleeping naked on his back. Tanya was lying on her side and had one hand draped across his chest. Brian walked to the dresser and put Lil Jay's pistol in his waistband, while Carmelo stood over Tanya. He made sure the windows and blinds were closed before turning on the light and standing over Lil Jay.

"Turn that fuckin' light out," Lil Jay said, covering his face with a pillow.

"I didn't turn it on," Tanya said, groggily.

"Who the fuck did then?"

"Oh shit!" Tanya yelled and tapped Lil Jay.

"What? What bitch? Stop hitting me!" Lil Jay pulled the pillow away from his face and stared down the barrel of Brian's gun. "Fuck!"

"You know the routine," Brian told him from behind the bandana. "Easy or hard? Quick or slow? Live or die? We want the money and the dope in exchange for your life. Every lie you tell, you'll pay for it. Understand?"

"Yeah," Lil Jay said, reluctantly.

"Now, turn over and put your hands behind your back," Brian instructed.

Brian took handcuffs off his waist and put them around Lil Jay's wrist. When Lil Jay was cuffed, Carmelo took the pair Brian had given him and looked at Tanya.

"The easy way or the hard way?" Carmelo told her.

Tanya put her arms in front of her and Carmelo put the cuffs on.

"Where's the money?" Brian asked Lil Jay.

"What money?"

Brian took the pistol from his waist and in one quick motion, slapped Lil Jay across the face. Two of Lil Jay's teeth flew out of his mouth and blood gushed down his face.

"When I ask you something, do not lie to me," Brian said to Lil Jay without an ounce of remorse. "Now, I'm going to ask you one last time, where is the fucking dope and money?"

"I swear," Lil Jay cried, "I don't have no dope!"

"Then, where the fuck is the money at?" Brian demanded.

When Lil Jay hesitated again, Brian grabbed the sock. "Open wide."

Lil Jay pleaded for his life as Brian put the sock in his mouth.

"Are you going to tell us where the dope and money are?" Brian asked again.

When Lil Jay put his head down, Brian grabbed the knife off the dresser and sliced Lil Jay from ear to cheek. Lil Jay yelled into the sock, tears rolling down his face, and he shit and pissed all at the same time. Tanya scrambled to the other side of the bed as Carmelo stood there.

Brian lifted Lil Jay's head up by his hair.

"Are you going to tell us where the shit is or not?"

Slowly Lil Jay nodded his head. Brian took the sock out of Lil Jay's mouth.

"Where?"

Lil Jay nodded toward the closet.

Carmelo walked into the closet and saw at least seventy to eighty pairs of shoes and just as many outfits. He looked at Brian.

"Where?"

"In the shoeboxes," Lil Jay muffled.

Carmelo took out every shoebox and started looking through them. He was down to the last six boxes when he found what they were looking for. The shoebox was filled with hundred-dollar bills. The next two were filled with twenty-dollar bills, the one after that had more hundreds, and the last two were filled with fifty-dollar bills.

"We're good," Carmelo said as he walked to the bed and grabbed a pillow.

"Nah. I still don't have the dope," Brian said and looked at Lil Jay. "I'm giving you one last chance to tell me the truth or I'm going to cut your dick off and put it in your asshole, nigga. One chance. Now, where is the dope?"

"I have two kilos in my daughter's room," Lil Jay finally admitted.

"Where is her room?"

"Across the hall."

"Is she here?"

"No."

"Where at in her room?"

"Behind the dresser, taped on the inside. Just take the drawers out."

Brian motioned to Carmelo who left the room. He stood against the wall until Carmelo returned with the kilos.

"Now, we're ready."

Carmelo put the two kilos in the pillowcase with the money and walked to the door. He turned around and looked at Brian.

"Go wait in the car," he said, and Carmelo left.

# Chapter 6

---

# Bunny

"You got some place to go tonight?" Brian asked Carmelo as they dumped the stolen car and got into his truck.

"Huh?"

"Do you have some place to go tonight?"

"Yeah, a few places."

"Are they awake this time of night?"

"What time is it?"

"1:58."

"Yeah, take me to Bunny's pad, she's woke," Carmelo said and gave Brian the address. He knew that even if Bunny wasn't awake, the window was unlocked.

Bunny was one of the females Carmelo had gotten pregnant. She was brown skinned with pretty brown eyes. Not skinny, but just the right size, with nice titties and a round ass. She was considered a dime piece by hood definition and Carmelo had her. He felt lucky because she wanted to be with him even though he didn't have shit. Her only flaws were, she had the mouth of a sailor, smoked weed and cigarettes, and gang banged like a nigga.

"All of the lights are out," Brian said as they pulled in front of the house.

"Yeah, but the window is open," Carmelo assured him.

"You gon' be good?"

"Yeah, my nigga."

"We'll deal with all this shit tomorrow," Brian told Carmelo. "Are you going to be here?"

"Yeah."

"You did good tonight, my nigga. Trust me and you'll never be broke again," Brian grabbed a pen and paper out the middle console and wrote down his pager number.

"What's your number?" Brian asked.

Carmelo told him before exiting the vehicle.

As Brian drove away, he thought about the robbery and how smooth Menace had been through the whole thing—calm, quiet, and no extra shit. He liked the lil' nigga and didn't mind splitting the money three ways. He just hoped that the nigga wouldn't get flashy and spend all his money at one time or let them niggas he called friends use him now that he had money. As he pulled in front of his own home, Brian made a decision, he would teach Menace the game.

# Chapter 7

## Brian

Carmelo crept through the window, making sure not to make any noise. Bunny slept in a pair of panties and a t-shirt. Even with the fan on high, she had the covers off and the t-shirt was around her waist. Carmelo stared at her and wondered what type of mom she would be and if the baby would slow her down. *Time would tell.* Right now, he was tired and all he wanted to do was sleep.

Carmelo took off his clothes and laid down. Bunny stirred, turned over, and looked at him.

"Hey, baby," she smiled.

"Hey."

"You just got here?"

"Yeah."

"What time is it?"

"After two."

"Why you come over so late?"

"We'll talk about it tomorrow, baby. Go back to sleep."

Carmelo laid on his back and stared at the ceiling. Bunny put her head on his chest and fell asleep.

Carmelo woke up feeling good and it wasn't because of what happened last night. He opened his eyes and saw Bunny's mouth on his dick.

"I knew this would wake you," Bunny said, then stared at him while she held his dick in her hand.

She licked the head first, going around in circles, making Carmelo's dick jump. She kept her eyes on him the whole time, just the way he liked it. Then she held her tongue out and licked his dick from the base to the head, never losing eye contact.

"You like?" she teased, toying with him.

After she felt like he could take it no longer, she took him in her mouth. Carmelo put his head back and enjoyed the moment. She did something with her mouth and tongue that made Carmelo open his eyes and look at her. She kept sucking and squeezing his balls.

*At seventeen, she knows how to blow a nigga's mind, literally*, Carmelo thought to himself.

Bunny increased her motion, up and down, up and down, up and down, and Carmelo arched up, feeling himself about to cum. Bunny took her hand and grabbed the base of his dick and started jerking it to match her mouth's rhythm.

"Oh shit," Carmelo said on the verge of cumming. "Oh shit."

Bunny didn't stop as Carmelo came in her mouth. He laid there, exhausted. After a moment he heard the water running in the bathroom and Bunny gargling. She came back into the room, jumped on the bed, and kissed him.

"Baby, are you hungry?"

"Yeah." Carmelo sat up and reached for his boxers.

"What do you want to eat?"

"It doesn't matter," he answered honestly.

"Do you want some pancakes?"

"Yeah. And bacon too."

As she got up to leave the room Carmelo stopped her. "Where's Moms at?"

"She's already left."

"What time is it?"

"A little past noon," Bunny told him.

"Damn," Carmelo said as he put on his boxers and headed for the bathroom.

He closed and locked the door. As he was getting out of the shower Bunny knocked on the door.

"Your food is done. Why is the door locked, nigga? I told you that my mom was gone."

"Because of your badass sister," Carmelo said, opening the door.

"Beatrice isn't here. It's just us, baby," Bunny said laughing.

Carmelo wrapped the towel around him and sat at the kitchen table. Bunny placed a glass of Kool-Aid and a plate with pancakes and bacon in front of him and walked away. Carmelo ate his food and watched Bunny move around the kitchen, washing dishes and wiping down counters. It was at that moment he realized how good of a woman he had. She treated him like a king. She sold weed for a hustle and spent her money on him. She ironed his clothes and cooked his food. She was a good girl, and now, he'd be able to pay her back.

"Where were you last night?" Bunny asked, sitting in the chair next to him.

"Why?"

"Because I paged you, but you never called back."

"My fault. I had a lot on my mind."

"Like what?"

"It doesn't matter, today is a new day," Carmelo said as he finished his food. He got up, about to put his plate in the sink, when Bunny grabbed it.

"I got it," Bunny said. "You just go get dressed before my momma walks through that door."

Carmelo went into Bunny's room and got dressed. He had just put on his shirt when his pager went off. He grabbed it, looked at the number, and picked up the phone.

"Hello."

"Yeah, somebody paged?"

"What's up, lil' nigga, it's me."

"What's up, B-Dog?"

"You dressed?"

"Yeah."

"Are you still at Bunny's house?"

"Yeah."

"I'm on my way."

"Cool," Carmelo said and hung up.

"Who was that?" Bunny asked as she walked into the room.

"That was the homie," Carmelo said as he reached down and grabbed his pistol.

"What you finna do?"

Carmelo laughed as he watched Bunny's look. He walked into the bathroom and started brushing his teeth. Bunny followed him.

"How long are you going to be gone for?" Bunny asked. She hated being ignored.

"I don't know."

"Are we ever going to spend time together?" Bunny put her hands on her hips.

"We just did, and I loved every minute of it," Carmelo said and smiled.

Bunny punched him in the arm. "I'm serious. Ever since I told you I was pregnant; it seems like you've been avoiding me."

Carmelo looked at Bunny and pulled her close to him. "Baby, I love you, and I'm glad that you're having my baby. I'm not trying to avoid you. I'm trying to be a man and make ends meet for us. You can't feed a baby off of love."

"Carmelo," Bunny began, "I have money and so does my mom. We're going to be alright. This baby will be fine." A horn honked outside interrupting their conversation.

Carmelo kissed Bunny long and hard. "I love you, but that's my baby in your belly, not your mom's and not yours alone. So let me do what I got to do to take care of both of y'all. Okay?"

The horn honked again. "Okay?" Carmelo asked again.

"Okay."

"I gotta go. I'll see you later," Carmelo said, rushing out of the door.

"I love you too," Bunny whispered as the door closed.

# Chapter 8

# Tanya

"What's up, nigga?" Brian greeted Carmelo.

"Shit," Carmelo pulled out a Newport and lit it.

"Blow that shit out the window," Brian demanded and shook his head.

They drove around in silence and listened to music.

"You hungry?" Brian asked as they pulled into McDonald's drive thru.

"Nah, I just ate."

Brian ordered enough food to feed a family and Carmelo looked at him.

"It's for my cousins too," he assured Carmelo and grinned.

Brian parked in front of a house by Lake Calhoun and got out.

"Come on," He said, and Carmelo followed.

Brian knocked on the door and a few seconds later Tanya answered. She saw Brian first and then Carmelo. Her face turned up, then she turned around and walked away.

"Lock my door," she yelled over her shoulder.

The house Tanya lived in was decked out. She had a white living room set with a 50-inch television and stereo system. Her dining room was all brass and glass. Brian, Tanya, and a little girl sat at the table eating.

"Come on over and eat with us," Brian instructed.

Carmelo sat at the table and grabbed a sandwich.

"Cousin Brian, who is that?" the little girl asked.

"His name is Menace, Jamie."

"That's a funny name," she said and eyed Carmelo.

When Jamie finished her food, Tanya looked at her. "All right, Jamie, go to your room and play, mommy will be up in a minute."

"All right, Mommy," the little girl said. "Bye, Cousin Brian." She waved at Carmelo and headed upstairs.

Carmelo and Brian burst into laughter.

"Four going on forty," Tanya said and shook her head. "Let's go to the basement."

When they were downstairs, Carmelo walked into a small room and saw a table with three neat piles of money on it. There were two large piles and a smaller one with two kilos of dope and six handguns next to it.

"This is what we hit for last night," Brian told them. "A little over four hundred and thirty thousand dollars."

Carmelo couldn't believe what he was seeing.

"Menace!" Brian called, shaking Carmelo from his daze.

"What's up?"

"Have you ever sold dope?"

"Yeah," Carmelo lied. The only dope he ever sold were peanuts wrapped in plastic.

"Have you ever cooked dope?"

"Nope."

"The two big piles of money are for me and Tanya. The little pile is for you."

Carmelo looked from Brian to Tanya.

"You want to know why?" Brian asked.

"Why?" he asked, although he didn't care.

Yesterday he had nothing and today he had more money than he'd ever seen.

"Because Tanya doesn't sell drugs, and I don't need to. Plus, with all the shit you're going through, the dope money is more of a guarantee. There's too much of a hit and miss with robbing."

Carmelo couldn't help but grin.

"So, we're giving you seventy-five thousand, two kilos, and six guns 'cause you're really going to need them."

"Okay."

Tanya grabbed one of the bags on the table and put her money in it. Carmelo and Brian followed suit.

"We good?" Tanya asked when the table was empty.

"We're good," Brian answered, then they looked at Carmelo.

"We're good," Carmelo said.

"Good. Now, get out of my house," Tanya said, climbing the stairs.

# Chapter 9

---

# Brian

"**D**o you have a place to put that shit?" Brian asked when they got into the truck.

Carmelo thought about it. He couldn't keep it at his stepmom's place, there were too many vultures there. Crystal and Bunny both stayed with their mom, and Jenny slept in the basement of a dope house.

"No," Carmelo said after carefully considering the question.

"I have an apartment that I usually bring hoes to," B-Dog told him. "I'm going to let you stay there for a while. Nobody comes over. Not your girlfriends, not your homies, nobody . . . I'm going to teach you how to cook that shit up, and once you know how to do that, you'll be good."

"Okay."

"You're young, so niggas are going to be jealous of you, and bitches are going to try to set you up. Don't be a fool. Them niggas in the hood that ain't on shit are going to try to leech off of you. Beware of the Dogs. Don't trust anybody because everybody has an agenda, a reason for fucking with you. Find that out so you can better deal with them. Everybody's not bad, but when you see bad in a person, don't forget it. Do good to those who deserve it, your family and your kids, 'cause in the end, that's who you'll see. Always think before you act, and don't put yourself in a position to lose. You don't want to find yourself in prison for life or dead because you let your heart lead you instead of your head." Brian knew the young nigga didn't understand a lot of the shit he was saying. He just hoped that one day he'd get it.

"Grab your shit," he told Carmelo when they got to the fourplex. Carmelo grabbed his bag and followed Brian into the apartment. "Put your bag in the back room. Tomorrow we'll go shopping."

Carmelo walked into the room and sat his bag on the floor. This felt like a new beginning. *I was broke not even twenty-four hours ago, and now look at me.*

"You ready?" Brian asked from the doorway, interrupting his thoughts.

"Yeah," Carmelo said and stood to leave.

"Grab some money, nigga," Brian told him. "You're not broke anymore."

Carmelo grabbed some money out of the bag and was about to count it but thought against it. He put the money in his pocket and turned out the light as he left the room.

When he walked into the living room, he could see that Brian was on the phone.

"Yeah, we're about to come through now . . . uh huh . . . uh huh . . . All right, we'll be there in ten minutes at the most . . . All right. One." Brian hung up the phone and looked at Carmelo. "Let's go."

They pulled into the projects in North Minneapolis off Olson Highway. It was the home of the Laos Boys, the Asian Bloods.

"What I'm showing you nobody else knows about, so keep it that way," Brian said as he parked.

"My homie, Johnny B, is going to take your flick and get you a fake ID so you can move around. We're going to get you your license, your own apartment, the whole nine. Just don't fuck it up. Okay?"

"All right."

Carmelo could count at least eleven Asians in front of Johnny B's house wearing either red bandanas, red Chuck Taylors, or red clothes.

He looked on the roof and saw an Asian with a red bandana around his face and one wrapped around an AK-47.

Carmelo put his hand on the butt of his gun but knew it was no use. The chopper would tear him and Brian down before he got a chance to pull it. *What is this nigga thinking? He makes me rich and gets me killed on the same day?*

Brian got out of the truck and stood in front of it until a short Asian man dressed in a red 'B' hat, no shirt, black shorts with a red belt, and red slippers walked out of the house. He said something in Laos and his homeboys relaxed. The Asian on the roof disappeared and Carmelo watched as the two shook hands and embraced.

"Damn, Blood," Brian said, "I would have thought you were the president of the United States or something the way you're protected."

"To them, I am," Johnny B said, and they laughed.

Brian looked at Carmelo and motioned for him to get out of the truck.

"Johnny B, this is my lil' homie, Menace," Brian said, and Carmelo extended his hand. "Menace, this is Johnny B, the Asian homie."

"Let's go inside," Johnny B told them.

From the outside, the house looked small. On the inside, it felt even smaller. The house was filled with Asian men and women. Some were sitting on the two couches in the living room, some sat on the floor, and the rest were standing. There were two kegs of liquor and weed on the table and rap music played on the television.

The three of them made their way to the backroom and Johnny B closed the door.

"So, you said that you needed another ID?" Johnny B asked Brian.

"Yeah, for my lil' nigga."

"You got the money?" Johnny B asked, all business.

"Yeah," Brian pulled out a wad of cash and handed it to Johnny B.

"Come on."

Carmelo followed Johnny B to another room where he took a few pictures of Carmelo from different angles.

For the next week, Carmelo became Brian's student. He learned how to cook dope and weigh it.

Carmelo sat in bed and thought about his life. He had everything he wanted, with enough money to do everything he needed to do. He was going to give Jenny, Crystal, and Bunny money for the babies, get an apartment so he wouldn't have to deal with the crowded house he slept in, enjoy his birthday, and look fly for school.

For Carmelo, B-Dog was the nigga who made it all happen, and the nigga he would be loyal to first.

# Chapter 10

# Carmelo

Carmelo woke to birds chirping. The window next to him was wide open and the blinds were up. *Damn, what time is it?* He got out of bed and walked to the living room. 11:03 a.m.

Carmelo was in the backroom counting his money when he heard somebody fumbling with the lock. He grabbed the pistol off the bed and crept into the hallway. Brian told him he brought hoes over but never told him any of them had a key. He crouched down and pointed the pistol at the door, waiting to see who it was. When Brian appeared with two bags from McDonald's, Carmelo lowered his gun. Brian saw Carmelo kneeling with the gun at his side and shook his head.

"What the fuck, nigga?" Brian said. "I told you nobody stayed here but me."

"I know, but I thought you were in the room sleeping. I didn't know who the fuck was opening the door," Carmelo explained.

"I've been up since eight this morning," Brian said as he sat the food on the table.

"What time are we leaving?"

"Are you ready to go shopping?"

"Hell yeah! I'm tired of wearing the same clothes," Carmelo said enthusiastically. "We're going to Foot Locker first, so I can get rid of these torn-down ass Nikes."

They spent the entire day shopping, going from store to store. Carmelo bought everything he liked and some things he didn't.

"How much money do you have left?" Brian asked when they were done.

Carmelo reached in his pocket and counted his money. "Forty-eight dollars. Why?"

"'Cause after we drop these clothes off, we're going to Old Country Buffet and you're buying," Brian told him, and Carmelo laughed.

As they were bringing the bags into the house, Brian got a page.

"Damn, this nigga's done that quick?" he said out loud as he headed for the phone.

Carmelo grabbed the rest of the bags from the truck and put them in the room.

"Dog, you ready?" Carmelo asked after he came from the bathroom.

"Yeah, somebody is about to drop something off first, then we'll be ready to go."

Carmelo showered again and dressed in his new clothes. When he came out of the room, Johnny B and another Asian were walking into the house.

"What's up, Blood?" Brian greeted Johnny B.

"Shit," Johnny B said and the two of them shook hands. "What's up, Menace?"

"What's up?"

"Are you ready to be legal?" Johnny B asked.

"Hell yeah," Carmelo said with a Kool-Aid grin on his face.

Johnny B handed Carmelo an envelope with two cards inside. One was a Minnesota Driver's License, the other a Social Security Card.

Carmelo looked at the driver's license for a while, not believing his eyes. *Micheal NMN Wilson.*

"Good looking, Johnny B."

"No problem, B."

Brian looked at Johnny B. "Good looking, Blood. Let me know if you need me."

"You do the same."

"You ready to eat?" Brian asked after Johnny B and his homie left.

"Hell yeah!" Carmelo went into the room and grabbed the wallet B-Dog told him to buy earlier, put the IDs in it, and headed for the door. Life was getting better every day.

# Chapter 11

---

# Carmelo

Carmelo woke early the next morning and walked into the living room. Brian was sitting on the couch eating cereal and watching TV.

"What time is it?"

"8:07."

"Damn, it's early as fuck," Carmelo said and stretched.

"Get on up so we can go grab you a car and get you moving."

Hearing the word 'car', Carmelo became alert. He went to the bathroom and showered. He got dressed, counted out seven thousand dollars, and left the room.

"Baby, I'll be home in a few hours, alright . . . We'll deal with it then . . . uh huh . . . uh huh . . . alright . . . I love you, too." Brian hung up the phone and looked at Carmelo. "You ready?"

"Yeah."

"I'm taking you out to the suburbs to get a ride," Brian told him as they drove towards the highway. "The cars are nicer, and the people are easier to deal with.

"Be conscious of your surroundings and who you let into your car because it's registered in your name. That fake ID is for your benefit, for you to escape, so be responsible. That's your freedom so don't trap yourself on both sides. Your alias is your alias. It's not for your bitches to know, your family, or your niggas. Don't ever tell anybody where you got your ID from, who you got it from, nothing. So basically, keep it hidden. If you're going to do dirt, leave your ID and anything tied to that name at home. Get you a nice lil' pad away from everybody for you to hide out at just in case the hood gets too hot."

Brian and Carmelo stared at one another.

"I gave you all that I can give you," Brian broke the silence. "It's your turn to either fuck the world or let it fuck you."

# Chapter 12

## Jenny

Carmelo got off the highway on the 35th/36th exit and took two rights. He stopped in front of the spot where Jenny was staying on 34th and 1st. She lived in a dope spot for the past five months with her dad's friend Harry. Her dad had kicked her out of the house once he learned that she dated Black men. At eighteen and five foot seven, blond hair and blue-eyed, Jenny was an outcast to her family. She and Carmelo had been seeing one another for the past six months, and now she was pregnant.

Carmelo knocked on the door.

"Who is it?"

"It's Carmelo, open the door."

Elnora, one of the fiends who lived there, opened the door.

"What's up, C-Melo?" she asked as he walked into the house.

"Shit, Elnora. Where's Jenny?"

"Downstairs locked in her room."

Jenny stayed in the basement of Harry's house. She had a lock on the outside and inside of the basement door to protect herself and her shit. You could never trust a fiend. Carmelo knocked on the basement door. When no one answered and he saw that it was locked he knocked harder.

"Who is it?" Jenny yelled.

"It's me, baby. Come open the door."

Carmelo heard Jenny coming up the stairs. The door opened and Jenny stood there in a red bra and panty set.

"Hey, baby! Where have you been?" she asked, throwing her arms around him.

"Come here," he said and held her.

"Oh, I missed you so much, Carmelo. I didn't know what happened to you. You weren't answering your pages, and your family hadn't heard from you . . ." her voice trailed off as tears welled in her eyes.

"I'm here now, baby," he said, trying to comfort her. He kissed her on the forehead, then her cheek, and then her lips. "Come on."

Carmelo led her down the stairs and to the bed. He hadn't had pussy all week and was hard as a rock. They undressed in a rush.

"Lay back," Jenny told Carmelo and he did as she asked.

She got on top of him, grabbed his dick, and guided it into her pussy. She was tight and soaking wet. She began riding him, moving her hips front to back, slowly at first, and then a little faster. She had her hands on his stomach, her pink nipples hard like two little buds.

"Oh yes! Oh, Carmelo . . ." she moaned as she rocked from front to back, riding his dick. Jenny started lifting up on her way back, coming down on his dick as she moved forward. Carmelo felt good. Jenny knew how to fuck.

Carmelo put his hands on her hips. Up and back. Down and forward. Every time she came down on his dick, he would lift his pelvis up giving her all dick.

"Oooh . . ." she moaned. "Oooh . . . oh, Carmelo . . . Don't stop . . . oooh."

Jenny sat up straight then leaned back and grabbed Carmelo's calves.

She was squeezing her pussy muscles and it felt so damn good. He reached down and touched Jenny's clitoris and she came.

"Oooh, Carmelo . . . Ooh . . . oooh . . . oooh . . . Don't stop," she moaned. Her pussy contracted and squeezed until her orgasm subsided.

"Oooh, baby. That felt good."

"Get up."

"Huh?" she asked, confused.

"Turn over. It's my turn to cum."

Jenny turned around and got into the doggy-style position. Carmelo grabbed his dick and rubbed it against Jenny's pussy lips.

"Aaah," she moaned.

He entered her, slowly at first, pumping in and out, controlling the tempo. Jenny opened her legs a little wider and arched her back, allowing Carmelo more of her. He grabbed a handful of her hair and increased his strokes. Pounding his dick in and out.

"Play with your clit," Carmelo commanded, and Jenny licked her fingers and began rubbing her clitoris.

"Oooh . . . oooh, Carmelo. I'm about to cum. I'm about to cum, baby!"

When Carmelo felt Jenny's orgasm, he began fucking her hard and fast, slamming his stomach into her ass with each pump.

When she climaxed for a second time, Carmelo couldn't take it any longer. He came hard inside of Jenny and then fell onto the bed, exhausted. Jenny laid next to him and after a while turned over to face him.

"Oh, I missed you, Carmelo."

"I missed you too, baby. It was for a good cause though."

"What are you talking about?"

"As long as you're pregnant, you can't sell dope."

"You think that it's going to hurt the baby?" she asked with concern.

"I don't know, but I'm not taking any chances."

"So, how do we live?"

"Let me worry about that," he told her. "How much money do you have?"

"Around seven hundred dollars, why?"

"Quit asking so many damn questions and just listen. I need you to start looking for an apartment for us."

"What kind of an apartment are you trying to get for seven hundred dollars?" she asked realistically.

"I'm going to give you twenty thousand dollars. Tell the landlord that you need to move in by the first and let him know that you have the first and last month's rent with you now."

Jenny looked at Carmelo with disbelief. "So, you're going to give me twenty thousand dollars?"

"That's what I said. And I need you to get on that a-sap. Get up, so we can shower and get you looking."

After they showered and dressed, Carmelo grabbed the bag with the money in it and set it on the bed.

"Where did you get this money from?" Jenny asked.

"It doesn't matter," Carmelo said. "That's twenty thousand right there. Take five and put the rest up, okay."

"Okay."

"I gotta go," Carmelo said and stood.

"Me too. I'm going to go grab The Star Tribune and look for an apartment now," Jenny said as she put the ziplock bag with the money inside of her purse.

They left the basement and Jenny locked the door.

"Baby, do you need me to drop you off somewhere?" she asked when they were outside.

"Nah," Carmelo told her. "I have my own G-Ride."

"Where?"

"Right there," he said and pointed at the Lincoln Continental parked three cars from hers.

"You're shitting me," Jenny said, wide-eyed.

"I'm not. Focus on the apartment, baby and get us from over here," Carmelo said and kissed her.

He walked toward the Lincoln, knowing that she was watching. Carmelo got in and turned the music up, put the car into drive, and pulled off, leaving Jenny standing on the sidewalk. Carmelo rode past her, nodded, and then sped down 1st Avenue. He was headed to see the love of his life, Crystal.

# Chapter 13

---

# Crystal

Crystal lived in the Bogus Boy neighborhood, so Carmelo rode with the pistol on his lap. He had murdered a Bogus Boy member at the beginning of the year and kept his gun within arm's reach, just in case.

Carmelo parked in front of Crystal's apartment complex and walked to the door. He pressed her apartment number and put his hand near his waist and close to his gun. When no one answered, he was about to turn around and walk away, then he saw Crystal coming down the stairs.

"So, you can't return my page?" she asked, opening the door. "You had me worried something happened to you, Carmelo. I was so scared I called your momma's house."

"Do you feel better now?" Carmelo asked, staring into her eyes.

"That look ain't going to cut it," Crystal said, angrily.

"Can I at least get a hug?" Carmelo asked and put his arms around her. Crystal was reluctant at first, but when she put her arms around him, she held on.

"I'm okay, baby," he whispered in her ear and she released him.

"Start answering your pages, Carmelo!"

"Where are you headed?" Carmelo asked, changing the subject.

"I have to go downtown and run this errand for my mom."

"Come on, I'll take you."

"Huh?" Crystal asked, shocked.

"I said that I'd take you."

"How? You gon' carry me, Carmelo?"

"Nah, I'm going to drive you," Carmelo told her and showed her the keys to the Lincoln.

"You don't own a car, and I'm not getting into a stolen one." Crystal placed her hands on her hips.

"Baby, the car isn't stolen, it's mine. I bought it today."

"How? You ain't got no money, so how did you buy a car?" she asked, looking him up and down. "What did you do?"

"Huh?"

"I said, what did you do? You're wearing new clothes, new shoes, and driving a car? Carmelo, we're about to have a baby. I can't raise this baby by myself." She was near tears.

"Crystal, you know that I love you more than anything in the world, right?" he looked at her, and she nodded her head. "And I would never do anything to cause you any hurt or pain. I'm sorry for disappearing on you last week, but it was necessary. It was for us, for our baby, for our future. I'll never leave. Do you believe me?"

"Yes, I believe you."

"Then let me take you downtown. Come on and get in the car."

Carmelo put his arm around her waist, and they walked to the car. He drove Crystal to run her errands. They talked and laughed and enjoyed one another's company. When she was done, Carmelo took her to lunch.

"I like this new Carmelo," Crystal told him as they waited for their food.

"This is just the beginning," he said, smiling.

They stood in silence for a while.

"What's on your mind?" Carmelo asked.

"I don't want anything to happen to you."

"I'm good."

"I see you in your car, these clothes, the money. I don't know what you're doing, just be careful. I need your help in raising this baby," Crystal said with sad eyes.

"I'm not going anywhere."

After they were done eating, they walked back to his car.

"I have a present for you," he said and reached into his bag.

"What is it?" she asked, excitedly.

He pulled out the ziplock bag and handed it to her.

"What the fuck is this?" she asked, surprised.

"It's for our baby. Our future," Carmelo told her. "Put it in your purse and hold on to it."

Crystal put the money in her purse, sat back in the car, and thought that this day couldn't be more perfect.

"Stop at Super America, baby, I need to grab something," Crystal asked as Carmelo drove down LaSalle.

When Crystal got out, Carmelo reached into his pocket for his cigarettes. He saw he only had three left and went into the store. Crystal was at the cash register and there were people in between them. After she paid for her items, she stood next to Carmelo.

"What you getting?" she asked in a playful voice.

"I gotta grab some gum," he lied. "Go wait in the car for me." Carmelo kissed her and she left the store.

A pretty blond female stood at the cash register.

"Can I get a pack of Newport 100s?"

Carmelo pulled out his driver's license with a five-dollar bill.

"Do you have an ID, sir?"

Carmelo handed her his driver's license and the five-dollar bill. She looked at his ID and reached for the cigarettes.

# Chapter 14

---

# Casper

"Yo, Cuz, ain't that that nigga Menace?" Casper asked Six Shot as they waited at the red light.

"Where?" Six Shot asked.

"Right there, Cuz," Casper pointed. "Coming out of SA."

"Yeah, that's that bitch ass nigga," Six Shot said, spotting him.

"Where's the heat at, Cuz? I'm going to smoke his slob ass," Casper told Six Shot.

"Cuz, you know ain't no bullets in the heat. Where you think we're on our way to?" Six Shot said to him.

"Fuck, Cuz, I wanna smoke this nigga."

They watched as Menace pulled out of the Super America gas station and drove down Blaisdell.

"Follow that nigga, Cuz," Casper commanded Six Shot. "That nigga is going through our hood. I hope we see one of the homies . . ."

Six Shot got behind Menace.

♦ ♦ ♦ ♦

As Carmelo drove down Blaisdell Avenue, he kept looking in his rearview mirror and on the street. He knew where he was and that he had to get Crystal out of this neighborhood soon. His mom also stayed in the Bogus Boy hood and it had been months since he had seen her.

R. Kelly's "12 Play" was playing as Crystal sat beside him. She was looking out of the window, sightseeing as if she had never driven down Blaisdell before.

When Carmelo got to 23rd Street his stomach turned. *Fuck. Fuck. Fuck. Not today, not to fucking day.* He had just gotten everything he wanted. Now, he was in his car, under his new identity, with Crystal in the passenger seat.

If it had been Bunny or Jenny, he would have been cool, they understood his life. Crystal, on the other hand, was too pure, and that's what he loved most about her.

Carmelo had to come up with a plan and fast . . . McDonald's was just up ahead.

# Chapter 15

# Casper

"Where in the fuck are the homies when you need 'em?" Casper said as he and Six Shot watched Menace take a left on 24th Street.

"Cuz, this nigga is giving himself to us," Casper got amped.

By Menace taking a left, going deeper into their hood, Casper knew they were bound to see one of the homies. Then he turned into McDonald's parking lot.

The Bogus Boys had a spot on 26th and Blaisdell and all Casper had to do was wait there while Six Shot drove up the block and grabbed a strap.

When Six Shot took the right into McDonald's and saw Menace driving out of the other exit, he knew they had fucked up and showed their hand.

"That nigga is on us, Cuz," Six Shot said.

"So what, fuck that nigga, Cuz. Follow that nigga!" Casper yelled, jumping up and down in his seat. "We're letting that nigga know ain't no coming through this hood, Cuz, worry-free."

Six Shot took a right out of McDonald's and followed Carmelo.

◆ ◆ ◆ ◆

"Fuck!" Carmelo said as he saw the car following him.

"What?" Crystal asked, looking concerned.

"Nothing," Carmelo said and looked into the rearview mirror.

Crystal turned around thinking it was the police but didn't see a police car.

"Don't look back," Carmelo told her and opened the glove compartment, grabbing the Glock .9, and putting it on his lap.

"Oh shit, Carmelo. What are you doing?" Crystal asked, looking at the gun in his lap.

"Calm down, baby. It's nothing," Carmelo said, but Crystal was hysterical.

"Don't tell me to calm down, Carmelo, and don't tell me that it's nothing. Why the fuck do you have that gun in your lap, and who's following us?" she cried.

"Crystal, calm the fuck down!" he snapped. "You've got my fucking baby in your stomach so chill the fuck out. I'm going to take care of this."

They stopped at the red light on 28th and Nicollet. When the light turned, Carmelo waited until all the cars passed on the opposite side of the street before turning left. As he turned, he stuck his gun out of the window and pointed it at the car following them. The car was in the process of turning but kept straight after seeing the gun.

When Carmelo pulled in front of Crystal's apartment, she got out of the car and walked to the apartment door, not once looking back. Carmelo made sure she was inside the building before he drove away.

# Chapter 16

---

# Carmelo

Five minutes later, he stopped in front of Bunny's house. It was the middle of the day, so he figured she wouldn't be there. He knocked on the door and her mom let him in.

"Hey, Carmelo," she said and opened her arms.

"Hey, Ma, how are you doing?"

"I'm doing good. How are you doing?"

"I'm okay. Just came to check on your daughter."

"You can't expect no seventeen-year-old girl to be in the house in the middle of the day," she said with a smile. "And it's summertime."

"Yeah, I know," Carmelo returned the smile. "I'm going to page her and see where she's at."

He reached for the phone.

"She's been worried sick about you and said you haven't been answering your pager. Your family hasn't seen you either," Bunny's mom, Sandy, was saying. "You know that you at least have to leave a message with somebody to let them know you're safe."

"I know, Ma," Carmelo said, hoping to end the conversation. "I know."

"You're about to be a father, you can't be having Bunny stressed out."

"It won't happen again, Ma."

Sandy was about to continue preaching when the phone rang. *Thank God*, Carmelo thought.

"Hello?" Sandy said into the receiver. "Nah, someone else did . . . Hold on." Sandy handed Carmelo the phone.

"Hello?" Carmelo said as she walked away.

"Hey, baby."

"Where are you?"

"I'm at Fire's house, but I'm about to come home."

"Nah, go ahead and enjoy yourself. I got something I have to do. I'll be back tonight around nine or nine-thirty. Be here then."

"I haven't seen you all week, baby. I want to see you," Bunny whined.

"I promise, I'll be back tonight. Okay?" Carmelo said, soothingly.

"Okay," Bunny said, reluctantly. "I love you, baby."

"I love you, too."

"So, y'all made up, huh?" Sandy asked when Carmelo returned to the living room.

"You know how it goes, Ma," Carmelo said and headed for the door.

"Are you coming back tonight?"

"Yeah. I'll be back," Carmelo kissed her on the forehead and headed for the door.

"You be careful."

"I will," he said and closed the door.

Carmelo got in his car and headed to the apartment in Northeast.

# Chapter 17

---

# Six Shot

"Yeah Cuz, I fucked the shit out of that bitch last night."

"Where you see her at, Cuz?"

"Cuz, me and Roach were riding down Franklin and saw these two hoes, Tasha and Sharnell, at Total gas station. Cuz pulls up and we get to talking to the bitches."

Roach interrupted OE. "Cuz, why the bitch Sharnell get to acting hella stuck?"

"Yeah, she did, Cuz," OE said and laughed. "You were acting hella steezy too, dude."

"No, I wasn't, Cuz. Quit bullshitting," Roach said, defensively.

"On my momma, Cuz."

Six Shot sat on the steps and zoned Roach and OE out. He'd been mad ever since they saw that bitch ass nigga Menace. On Bogus, if he would have had one bullet, he would have gotten out of his car, and smoked that hoe ass nigga. He had a .40 on him now and wanted to use it badly. He made a promise that the next time he saw Menace he was going to smoke his bitch ass. Then he saw it.

◆ ◆ ◆ ◆

Carmelo sat across the street in the bushes on 31st and Pillsbury and listened to the men tell their story. He half-heard them because his eyes were trained on Six Shot. The nigga could have killed his unborn seed earlier today. If he didn't have respect for Crystal, he would have killed this nigga earlier.

He and B-Dog had taken six guns from Lil Jay and one of them was a Smith and Wesson .9 with a beam on it. Carmelo knew what he had to do. He had to set an example. He had to make sure that his kids and family were safe and eliminate all danger and harm.

He raised the Smith and Wesson and turned on the beam.

# Chapter 18

---

# Menace

Six Shot saw the red dot on his shoe and thought he was tripping. He turned to his right and saw Roach and OE talking to Casper and Syke. He looked across the street again, then down at his shoe, and didn't see anything.

A car drove past and from the reflection, it looked as if someone was hiding in the bushes, but once the light was gone, it was too dark to tell. Six Shot began watching the bushes, waiting for any type of movement.

*The homies play too much*, he thought as he took another swig of his 40-ounce beer. The red dot came back, but this time it was on his chest. He knew he wasn't trippin' and stood up.

"Who is that?" he yelled, and OE stopped talking.

"What's up, Cuz?" Syke asked.

"There's somebody in the bushes, Cuz," Six Shot told them.

They looked across the street and didn't see anything.

"Cuz, you're tripping," Casper said, and after a few seconds, began talking again.

Six Shot picked up his 40 ounce, took a swig, and began walking toward the street. He knew what he had seen and was almost to the curb when a figure in all black came from behind the bushes.

"Who is that, Cuz?" he asked as he reached for his gun.

"It's me, muthafucka," was the last thing Six Shot heard before he was killed.

♦ ♦ ♦ ♦

Carmelo shot Six Shot in the face twice, then pointed the gun toward the other three men. The beam was turned off, but his aim was good. He hit Roach in the leg and ass, then shot him in the back twice before he collapsed on the ground. Carmelo then shot Casper in the shoulder before he hid on the side of the building.

When the clip was emptied, Carmelo turned and ran towards Blaisdell. He hid his bike on the side of someone's house two blocks up and rode to Bunny's house. Carmelo climbed through the window, stripped down to his boxers, and got into bed. Bunny rolled over, put her arms around him, put her head on his shoulder, and closed her eyes.

♦ ♦ ♦ ♦

Casper sat in the hospital bed and watched as the doctor stitched his shoulder. He knew who shot him and killed Six Shot and Roach. He underestimated the nigga, and now, three of his homies were dead.

*You will pay for what you did nigga. If it's the last thing I do. I'm going to make sure you pay*, Casper thought to himself.

# Chapter 19

---

# Carmelo

On the first day of school, Carmelo woke with a smile on his face. He had never had too much of anything and knew he was going to shine. He had worn Pro Wings or nameless shoes his entire life, and his clothes came from either Marshalls or Kmart. The closest he had come to anything name brand were Reebok Classics. And only because they cost thirty dollars.

He wore a pair of brown Nautica shorts, a white Nautica t-shirt under a red and white Nautica button-down with a brown collar, and low top white and red Nike Huaraches. His braids were fresh, he wore a Nautica watch and a gold herringbone necklace.

Carmelo wanted to drive his car to school but knew it would be careless and doing too much, so he left it at Bunny's house.

Bunny wore black Girbaud shorts that were tight around her ass, a red and black Jordan shirt, with red and black Jordans. Her hair was in a ponytail with a red bandana holding it together.

Roosevelt High School was run by the Bloods, and when Carmelo walked in, he felt alive. He and Bunny walked to the common hang-out spot where the Bloods and most popular people were.

"What's up, Menace? Bunny B?" He-Man asked, walking toward them.

"Shit nigga, what's good?" Menace replied as he shook He-Man's hand.

"I bee you, nigga. You fresh as hell today."

Carmelo went down the line, shaking niggas hands and hugging the females. He and Bunny kicked it until the first bell rang and everybody had to head to class.

Carmelo's day was going good until lunch. His first two lunch periods were spent at Bill's Garden eating Chinese food and shooting dice. Carmelo made it back for the last one.

He was sitting at a table with He-Man, Dolomite, Stanky B, and Sandman when he saw his little brother, Carl going through the food line. Carmelo looked at Carl wearing clothes he had worn in the summer and approached him.

"What's up, Melo?" Carl asked when he saw his brother.

"Shit." Carmelo looked at Carl's tray. "That's all you want?"

Carl had a hamburger and milk on his tray.

"Yeah, I'm okay."

"Come on," Carmelo told him, and they walked to Carmelo's table.

"Who dis?" Stanky B asked as Carl sat down.

"My little brother, Carl," Carmelo said and introduced him to everyone. Then he turned his attention to Carl.

"What have you been up to?" Carmelo asked, watching Carl devour his burger.

"Nothing."

"Cathy didn't take you shopping?"

"No," Carl told his brother. "She told me next month, if she had enough money."

"Did everyone else get new school clothes?" Carmelo asked, already knowing the answer.

"Yep."

"Daddy didn't take you shopping or give Cathy money for you?"

"He said he didn't have any," Carl said as if it was okay.

Carmelo and Carl were half-brothers. They had the same dad as Cathy's six kids, but they treated Carl differently. Carmelo was raised with his siblings from birth and was looked at as an equal. Carl, on the other hand, was introduced to them two years prior at a family reunion, and they felt indifferent towards him. His dad had moved Carl to Minnesota in June so they could get to know one another. He dropped Carl off at Cathy's house, forcing him to live with his siblings, who treated him like an outcast.

As Carmelo watched Carl eat, he made up his mind and decided to raise Carl.

"How do you like school so far?" Carmelo asked his brother.

"It's cool. I got some good classes, and the teachers are alright."

"How much stuff do you have at Cathy's?"

"As far as what?"

"Clothes, personal stuff, whatever?"

"Not much. Just the clothes I came with."

"Okay. After school we're going shopping," Carmelo said, and Carl's face lit up. "Meet me in the front after your last class."

"Okay, Melo," Carl said as the bell rang, informing everyone that lunch was over.

After school, Carmelo and Carl went shopping, and then to Jenny's apartment. He had already talked to Jenny, who didn't have a problem with Carl living with them.

"This is your room, nigga, so keep it clean," Carmelo told Carl as they stood in the spare room. "You make a mess; you clean it up. Never tell anyone where we stay, that includes family and Bunny. Alright?"

Carl looked around the room and grinned. "Okay."

# Chapter 20

---

# Brian

The next two months went by fast. Carmelo went to school when he could but had too many mouths to feed.

He took care of Jenny, Bunny, Crystal, and Carl, and even though he was able to provide for those he loved, he still felt broke. Yeah, he kept money in his pocket, but felt like he was only surviving, and not living. Something had to give and quick because this wasn't cutting it. His pager went off.

What's up, my nigga?" Brian asked.

"Shit. What's up with you?"

"One arm short and not enough eyes," Brian said.

Carmelo sat up straight. "Where you at?" His adrenaline was already pumping.

"I'm at the spot," Brian said, referring to the apartment in Northeast.

"I'll be there in twenty minutes." Carmelo hung up.

Carmelo walked into the apartment and saw Brian sitting on the couch.

"What's up?" he said as Carmelo closed the door.

"Shit."

"You ready to make this money?"

"Does a lion chase a zebra when it's hungry?" Carmelo asked, and they both laughed.

"What did you bring?" Brian asked.

Carmelo pulled out the 17 shot .40 caliber pistol.

"That'll scare 'em, but it makes too much noise. And if they hesitate, we're shooting." Brian handed Carmelo a smaller pistol.

"A deuce five, Dog?" Carmelo asked, looking disappointed.

"Nah, lil' nigga, it's an 11 shot .380. It's small, doesn't make that much noise, and does the trick."

Carmelo put the .380 in his pocket and listened to the plan.

"Where's Tanya?" he asked when Brian finished.

"She's not in this one. It's just you and me."

Carmelo sat and wondered, *how in the hell B-Dog knows all these niggas with kilos of dope and hundreds of thousands of dollars.*

"Your pockets empty?" Brian asked.

"Yeah," Carmelo told him.

"Let's go get this money then," he said, and they left.

Brian parked the car and grabbed the black bag in between them. At the back of the apartment complex, they stood on the side of the building and put their ski masks on.

"Remember, no hesitation," Brian told Carmelo, who nodded his head.

The security door was broken and opened with no problem. The hallway was dark as they walked to the door. Brian knocked and waited on someone to answer.

"Who is it?" a man with a heavy accent asked.

Brian said something in Spanish, and they waited.

A few seconds later the door opened. The first thing the man saw was Brian's gun. He put his fingers to his lips and motioned the man into the apartment. The Mexican looked like he was in his mid-twenties. His shirt was off, and he had tattoos from his neck to his waist. On his stomach in bold letters read '*VATO LOCO.*' Carmelo kept the gun trained on his face as Brian went through the house. Another Mexican man and woman were in the apartment. Brian ordered them into the living room. He spoke Spanish to the three and no one responded. He repeated what he said again, and when no one responded, he looked at Carmelo, who shot the Mexican who had opened the door in the arm.

"Ah shit, *Vato*! You shot me!" he said, holding his arm.

Brian repeated what he said a third time in Spanish and waited a few seconds. When no one responded, he looked at Carmelo again, who shot the other Mexican man in the chest.

"Shit, *Vato*, what do you want?" the Mexican who was shot in the arm yelled.

Brian spoke to him in Spanish.

"It's under the bag in the trash can, *Vato*," he said in broken English.

Brian went to search for the trash can. He came back a few minutes later and spoke to the woman in Spanish. When she didn't respond, Brian shook his head and locked eyes with Carmelo who raised his gun toward the woman. Before he could pull the trigger, the Mexican man shot in the arm yelled in Spanish, and Brian left the room again.

When he returned, he sat the bag down and pulled a long piece of rope from around his waist. He tied the woman's hands together behind her back and headed toward the door. Carmelo grabbed the bags and followed, closing the door as they walked out.

After school the next day, Carmelo took Carl home and drove to Northeast.

"What's up, nigga?" Brian asked when Carmelo walked through the door.

"Shit, tired as fuck," Carmelo said and sat on the couch. "Dog, where in the hell did you learn to speak Spanish?"

"High school," Brain said and laughed. "I didn't know if I was ever going to use it. It was either Spanish or German, and I haven't met no nigga who wanted to speak German."

They watched TV for a while and then Brian got up and went into the dining room. Carmelo followed and saw that there were two piles of money on the table, one larger than the other.

"We hit for a hundred seventy-six thousand. I gave you the seventy-six thousand. The dope is in the back in a bag with the rest of the shit you already have."

"All right, my nigga," Carmelo said with a smile on his face.

"You're a smooth lil' nigga. I respect your reason for hustling. Some people do shit just to do it but have no purpose or goal, so they spend it as quickly as they get it, and then two weeks later it's just a story to tell. As long as you keep a reason for your hustle, I'll continue to help you grow and get to the next level."

# Chapter 21

---

# Carmelo

The winter went by quickly. Carmelo had a steady clientele that made him quit school altogether. In mid-March, Sandman was shot and killed by the Six-0's coming out of Webb's Barber Shop, in the heart of Blood hood. An hour later Tre Dog was shot four times standing in front of Cups on 38th and Chicago.

As Carmelo headed to the hood, he knew it was going to be a long summer. The Bogus Boys, Family Mob, and Six-0's had formed an alliance, and their mission was to kill the Bloods.

Carmelo let it be known a long time ago that he wasn't going to become a Blood, but knew he was already in the war. He wasn't about to sit back and let no nigga come into his neighborhood and kill all his childhood friends.

"You can't make money and war at the same time," Brian was saying. "I know they're the niggas you grew up with, but they chose that life. If you were a Blood, I'd be the first to give you a pistol my nigga, but if you keep making their problems your problems, they're going to turn you into one. You're out for longevity and are about to be a father. You have three babies about to be born within the next few weeks and you're taking care of your little brother. That's where your priorities lie. Your obligation is to them first, 'cause if you're dead or in prison, your whole empire crumbles. Then what's going to happen? You have a lot of innocent people's lives in your hands."

Carmelo sat and listened, not saying a word.

"I know that you're going to do what you're going to do. All I can say is do it by yourself if you do anything and keep this one to yourself."

Carmelo knew what he was referring to. Everybody in the hood knew he had killed a Bogus Boy, and that wasn't a good look.

"You're my nigga," Brian said and neither of them spoke for a minute.

"You hungry?" Carmelo finally asked, and they burst into laughter.

# Chapter 22

## Carmelo

On April 4th, Crystal went into labor and gave birth to a girl. A month later, Bunny gave birth to a boy and three days after that, Jenny gave birth to another girl.

Carmelo knew there wasn't enough time to sell dope and spend time with his kids and needed help.

He'd been sending Lil Cliff and DeWayne to the store and had them doing little things here and there.

DeWayne's mom had been on the streets whoring since Carmelo could remember, and Cliff's mom ran the streets like she was a teenager instead of an adult. Cliff's older sister watched him most of the time, or whenever he came home because he spent most of his time in the hood with DeWayne.

Carmelo had been at the spot for three days and was tired. It was a Friday, and he knew that Cliff and DeWayne were out of school. He went outside and saw them walking up the street.

"Come here," he motioned to them.

What's up?" Cliff asked.

"Go grab me a gyro and Tahitian Treat," Carmelo said, and handed Cliff a fifty-dollar bill. "Grab y'all something to eat too."

When they came back, Carmelo was in the house sitting on the couch.

"Sit down and eat with me," he told them.

"How old are you?" Carmelo asked Cliff.

"Thirteen."

"You thirteen too, DeWayne?"

"Yep," DeWayne said, stuffing his mouth full of fries.

"What do y'all know about selling dope?" Carmelo got right to it. He was too tired to baby these niggas.

"We know enough," Cliff said, confidently.

"Do y'all know how to sell dope?"

"Yeah," DeWayne answered. "You give a fiend a pill, and he'll give you your money."

Carmelo spent the next hour quizzing the two teens. He already made his mind up to teach them what B-Dog taught him.

"Do y'all want to make money?" Carmelo finally asked.

"Hell yeah!" they said in unison.

"What time do y'all have to be home?"

"By ten-thirty," Cliff said.

"Anytime," DeWayne told him.

"Kick it with me this weekend. I'm gonna show y'all the game, and then Monday y'all will be on your own. Cool?"

They both nodded their heads.

# Chapter 23

# Carmelo

Carmelo and his mom never really had a falling out. One day he felt like he didn't want to follow her rules and left. He stayed with his stepmom, Cathy, most of the time so his mom always knew where he was.

His parents never tried to come to see him, so Carmelo let them be. Ever since his kids were born, he had a different outlook on parenting and hoped that his mom felt the same way about him as he felt about not seeing his kids.

"What are you doing up so early, babe?" Jenny asked.

Colleen had been up half the night and had just gotten back to sleep. Jenny looked at the clock, 9:57 a.m. She didn't hear Colleen and wondered what was going on.

"I'm going to church," Carmelo told her, and she laid back down.

It had been a year since Carmelo saw his mom, and he was nervous. He couldn't remember the last time he had been to church, and chose to go on Mother's Day.

It was a little after eleven when Carmelo walked into the church.

"They said I wouldn't make it . . . They said I wouldn't be here today . . ." Carmelo heard a beautiful female voice come through the church's speaker.

"They said that I'd never amount to anything . . . But I'm glad to say . . . That I'm on my way . . ."

Carmelo was standing next to the usher when he and his mom locked eyes. She began crying. His aunt saw him as well and tears began to flow down her cheeks.

Carmelo looked around the church and saw his family and went to sit with them.

After the offering, members of the church surrounded the pulpit for the congregational prayer. Carmelo stood in between his mom and aunt, holding their hands as the Pastor prayed. After the prayer, they fellowshipped for a few minutes, giving him time to interact with his family.

The choir had one more song to sing when everyone was seated. Terry, the organ player, started the music, and Carmelo saw his aunt walk to the mic.

"Tragedies are commonplace . . . All kinds of diseases people are slipping away . . . Economies down, people can't get enough pay . . . As for me, all I can say is, thank you Lord for all You've done for me . . ."

The choir joined in singing the lyrics to "Thank You Lord" by Walter Hawkins as Carmelo felt the tears rolling down his cheeks. It felt so good, he didn't even try to stop them.

After church, Carmelo talked with his family.

"Happy Mother's Day to all of y'all!" Carmelo said as they walked outside the church.

"We're all going to the house for dinner if you want to come," his mom asked.

"Nah, I got something to do."

Carmelo loved his mom and hated hurting her feelings.

"I'll start calling more. I promise." Carmelo hugged his mom.

"You be careful out there. Your momma loves you. Always has, always will."

"I love you too, Momma," he said and then looked at Crystal.

"Can I take you home?" he asked, and she hesitated. She looked at him then at her daughter asleep in her arms.

"Your mom is going to take me." She kissed him and walked away.

He understood. He watched them leave and then walked to his car, alone. As he started his car and pulled off, that's how he felt, alone. Carmelo laid down that night and went to sleep with mixed feelings.

# Chapter 24

---

# Carmelo

The Minneapolis gangs were at war. There were twenty-three murders in May, so Carmelo decided to send Carl to Illinois for the summer. He and Chris dropped Carl off and spent two days in Kankakee.

"I want you to put me on," Chris said to Carmelo as they were pulling out of the gas station in Black River Falls, Wisconsin.

"What do you mean?" Carmelo asked, and Chris looked at him.

"Melo, don't play dumb with me, you know what I'm talking about. Dope, nigga."

"Why?"

Chris gave him a crazy look. "Why ask why, nigga? The same reason why you do it."

"If you need money, I'll give you some money."

"Nigga, I'm not your bitch. I'm your brother, and I need to make my own money, buy my own clothes, and do my own thing. You're not the only one who got tired of living in that house with grown muthafuckas leeching off of everybody else. That's bullshit, nigga.

We're always out of shit. LaShaunda's pregnant and this is bullshit," Chris complained.

Carmelo looked at his brother and thought about it. *The nigga is going to do it regardless.* "Are you ready for this lifestyle?"

"Hell yeah!" Chris answered without hesitation.

Carmelo decided to help Chris to eliminate the bullshit down the line. Plus, he could use somebody he could trust to grind with.

"Give me a few days," Carmelo told Chris when he dropped him off at home.

The next day Carmelo woke to see Jenny walking around the house wearing a pair of thongs and nothing else.

"I see you're happy somebody's gone," Carmelo said as he played with his daughter.

"I love Carl, but I like to be free in my own house."

"You have three months now to do it."

"And I won't miss a day," she said and walked toward him. "Now, hand me my baby, so I can feed her."

Carmelo handed Colleen to Jenny and then paged B-Dog.

"What's up, my nigga?" Brian asked when Carmelo answered the phone.

"Shit, just got back into town. Seeing what's up."

"Ain't really too much happening. About to go over to my sister-in-law's house for a barbecue."

"Yeah?"

"Yeah. What are you about to get into?"

"Shit. About to jump in this shower and find something to do."

"Call me when you get out. I want you to ride with me."

"Cool. One," Carmelo said and hung up the phone.

"Where are you going, babe? You just got back," Jenny asked when she saw Carmelo dressed.

"Baby, I have to take care of something, then I'm coming back." He paged B-Dog and waited for him to call back.

"You ready, nigga?"

"What's the address?" Carmelo wrote it down and hung up. He kissed Jenny and his daughter. "I'll be back in a few hours."

When Carmelo got to the house, he parked and sat for a minute. He paged B-Dog from his car phone and waited.

"Where you at?" Brian asked.

"I'm out front," Carmelo told him, and Brian disconnected the call.

A few seconds later, he came from the side of the house. Carmelo got out of the car and walked up the steps.

"This is a nice ass house."

"It's my sister-in-law's."

When they got to the backyard, Carmelo was in awe. The yard was huge, with a pool, a patio, a big garage, and a barbecue pit. He counted four females and five males, with no one looking over 21 besides B-Dog, who introduced Carmelo to everyone as Mike.

"Where are your sister-in-law and your wife?" Carmelo asked.

"In the house. You want to meet them?"

"Nah, they'll be coming out soon. I'll see 'em then."

# Chapter 25

# Maria

"Who is that boy Brian's talking to?" Maria asked Melinda.

"Some boy he's been spending a lot of time with," Melinda answered and peeked out of the window. "He doesn't look twenty-one, but he is cute."

"I hope Brian isn't trying to hook me up with one of his hoodrat ass friends again," Maria said.

"I told him to let you do your own searching. He hasn't tried in a while, so don't sweat it," Melinda said as they both stared out the window.

"What did you say his name was again?" Maria asked her sister.

"Huh? What?"

"What did you say Brian's friend's name was?"

"Why?" Melinda questioned.

"Just wondering."

"Mike something," Melinda said, watching Maria's reaction. Brian had told her that Maria would like him.

◆ ◆ ◆ ◆

"So, how are things going with you?" Brian asked, putting charcoal into the grill.

"Shit, I'm good. I got used to my brother Carl being there and thought I was going to be able to do me for a while, now my brother Chris wants me to put him on."

"What did you tell him?" Brian poured lighter fluid on the charcoal.

"What could I tell him? I told him that I'd holler at him in a few days," Carmelo said, and Brian looked at him.

"You're my nigga," Brian told Carmelo. "And I don't want new niggas in my business. What we do is for us. It's not for everybody."

"My nigga, I know that. I ain't finna let him know shit about nothing I'm doing. I'ma introduce him to Biz, let them deal with each other. Biz is a trustworthy nigga, so I know he ain't going to fuck my brother over. I got this," Carmelo said, reassuring Brian.

"I knew there was a reason I liked you," Brian said and took a swig of his beer. "Here they come now."

Carmelo turned and could not believe his eyes.

# Chapter 26

---

# Maria

"Grab the pan of meat, Maria," Melinda told her sister, but Maria didn't hear her. She was nervous. She'd been watching Mike and believed he was more than cute. She watched as he and Brian talked and got butterflies in her stomach when Mike smiled.

"Maria!" Melinda yelled and tapped her on the shoulder.

"What?" she asked, turning her attention to Melinda.

"Grab the meat and let's go, so we can eat."

Maria grabbed the pan and turned to her sister.

"How do I look?"

"You look beautiful," Melinda said sincerely, causing Maria to blush.

♦ ♦ ♦ ♦

Carmelo prayed to God that the female carrying the meat wasn't B-Dog's wife. The woman in front was pretty, with nice brown skin, long black hair tied in a ponytail, full lips, and beautiful, but looked older than the female behind her.

She had her hair parted in the middle and loose around her face. Even so, you could see the shape of it. She had big brown eyes, a small nose, and full lips.

He watched her talk and laugh with the guests, and thought to himself, he wouldn't want to see her any other way. She wore a black Nike t-shirt, blue jeans, and black Nike Air Maxs.

When the sisters got to the grill, the younger woman sat her pan of meat on the small table beside the grill, avoiding eye contact. Carmelo's heart was pounding a mile a minute as he stared at her. The moment their eyes finally met, he *knew* and believed that she did, also.

# Chapter 27

# Carmelo

Brian put his arm around his wife and kissed her on the forehead. He'd been burned too many times and didn't trust a lot of people, yet he trusted Carmelo with his life. He knew Carmelo and Maria would be a good match. He was too serious, and she was too naive. Carmelo could teach her, and she could make him happy.

"Yo, Mike!" Brian finally said, breaking them from their trance.

Carmelo looked away, embarrassed. "What's up?"

"This is my wife, Melinda." He introduced them and Carmelo nodded his head. "And this is her sister, Maria."

"Hi." He gave her his crooked smile.

"Hi." She replied and they stood there in silence.

"Maria, I need your help in the kitchen," Melinda said, breaking the awkwardness and carting her sister off.

◆ ◆ ◆ ◆

When they were out of earshot, Brian flipped the meat and looked at Carmelo. "My nigga, you kill people for a living and don't bat an eye. You shoot people and go eat afterward. Yet, you see a female and you freeze up? What the fuck is that?" Brian shook his head.

"You caught me off guard, nigga. You should have told me, and I would have been prepared," he said and looked at the door Maria went into. "Damn she's bad, Dog . . . You should have told me."

◆ ◆ ◆ ◆

"I'm so embarrassed," Maria said once she was safe in the kitchen. Melinda had only seen her sister act like this one other time, and that was ages ago.

"You didn't expect him," Melinda said, comforting her sister. "He was just as stunned by you as you were by him."

"Was he?" Maria asked, searching her sister's eyes for any kind of deceit.

"He likes you."

"Yes, I think that he does."

Maria got a cup and turned on the faucet. As the water ran, she looked out the window and watched him. Damn, she felt like a kid.

◆ ◆ ◆ ◆

"You good, nigga?" Brian asked Carmelo.

"Yeah."

"You straight?"

"Yeah," Carmelo said with a little more confidence.

"You focused?"

"Yeah," Carmelo was amped up now.

"You ready to holla at her?"

"Nah," Carmelo's confidence left, and Brian burst into laughter.

"Take this inside of the house," Brian said and handed Carmelo a pan full of cooked meat.

◆ ◆ ◆ ◆

Maria had her back to the window talking to her sister.

"I have to use the bathroom," Melinda told her and left.

Maria turned around, looking out of the window for Mike. When she didn't see him, she leaned on the kitchen sink to get a better view of the yard. *Where are you*, she thought, and heard the screen door open. She turned around expecting to see her niece or nephew and was shocked to see Mike standing there, holding a pan of meat.

"Brian told me to bring this in."

"You can set it on the table," Maria stuttered, her head instantly perspiring. Carmelo sat the pan down and faced her.

"I'm sorry about out there. My name is Mike," he said and extended his hand.

"Maria," she said, feeling herself getting moist as he held her hand.

# Chapter 28

# Brian

Three weeks later, Brian paged Carmelo.

"What's up, my nigga?"

"Where you at?" Brian asked.

"Where am I supposed to be?" Carmelo questioned, confused.

"We're at my house."

"What's the address?" he asked and memorized it. "I'm on my way."

Carmelo was anxious. He had been talking to Maria for the past three weeks on the phone but hadn't seen her. He knew she was there, and this was going to be their first face-to-face encounter since the barbecue.

When he parked in front of Brian's house, Carmelo couldn't believe his eyes. B-Dog stayed in a big ass house a block away from Lake Calhoun. He knocked on the door. Maria opened it to greet him.

"Hi Mike," she said and stepped aside, inviting him in.

"Is that all you got?" he asked and opened his arms. *Damn, she smells good,* Carmelo thought and squeezed her.

"I've missed talking to you on the phone," she told him.

"I've missed you, too."

She smiled. "I'm glad you came."

"Me too."

She gave him a peck on the lips and turned to go into the house, but he grabbed her hand.

"You don't do that and expect me to let you walk away. Close the door and get out here."

She closed the door, and they kissed passionately like they'd been lovers for years. When their lips parted, they stared at one another.

"Let's go inside before we get into trouble," she told him after a while.

"It's about time you came in," Brian said with a smile.

"Hi Melinda," Carmelo said, ignoring him.

"Hi, Mike. How are you doing?"

"I'm good," he answered and looked at Maria.

"The fireworks start at ten," Brian told them. "That gives us a lot of time to find something to do."

They walked to Applebee's for dinner and sat outside of Brian's house and watched the fireworks.

# Chapter 29

## Cliff & DeWayne

They saw him cut across Central Park and drove down 3rd Avenue. Not too fast, because they wanted to catch him slipping. He continued down 4th Avenue and when they made it to 4th Avenue, they spotted him and took a left. They sped up a little bit, but at the corner, he took a right and headed toward 5th Avenue. When they were turning right on 4th, he was turning left on 5th.

*This nigga must know we're following him because he's taking too many turns,* the driver thought and didn't care. The Bloods had killed his brother a week ago, and he was going to smoke one in retaliation.

He drove to the corner on 5th Avenue, saw the nigga get off his bike and walk into a house. He backed his car up and took a left through the alley.

◆ ◆ ◆

"What's up, my nigga?" Cliff asked as Carmelo walked through the door.

"Shit. What's up with y'all?"

DeWayne sat on the couch with a large rifle on the dining room table.

"What the fuck is that?" Carmelo asked DeWayne.

"It's a hundred shot .9mm Calico."

Carmelo put the bag of dope on the table and picked up the rifle.

"Y'all niggas got tired of them deuce fives, huh?" Carmelo asked DeWayne. "What did you pay for this?"

"An eight ball," DeWayne told him.

"What you gon' do with something like this, nigga?"

"The same thing you would," DeWayne told him, and Carmelo smiled.

"Sell it to me," Carmelo finally said.

"You're my nigga. If anything, I'd just give it to you."

"I don't want it like that." Carmelo reached into his pocket and counted out five hundred dollars. "Here you go."

DeWayne took the money and put it in his pocket.

"Take this too," Carmelo handed DeWayne the pistol he had on his waist.

"I got heat," DeWayne told him.

"I don't want to carry this big ass gun and a pistol. Hold it for me," Carmelo said and handed DeWayne the pistol.

Carmelo figured he'd ride to Bunny's and drop the Calico off. *What could happen to me on the way to Bunny's*, he thought.

Carmelo put the rifle in a duffel bag.

# Chapter 30

---

# Cliff & DeWayne

"Where's Cliff?" Carmelo asked.

"Outside."

"What's up, my nigga?" Carmelo asked Cliff when he saw him.

"Shit, tired as hell, but I'm good," Cliff replied.

"What's on your mind?"

"Just dealing with a lot of bullshit at home with my mom bringing all of these niggas to the pad, and my sister and her bullshit."

"If you need a place to stay for a while, let me know, I got you," Carmelo said sincerely.

"I'm good," Cliff said.

"Let me know if you need me," Carmelo told him and walked off the porch.

He grabbed his bike and was about to get on, but his pager went off.

Carmelo started walking, trying to figure out who's number it was, then DeWayne yelled his name. Carmelo knew the sound and fell to the ground.

Sysco and Fred got out of the car and left it parked in somebody's backyard with the engine running. *This will be quick,* Sysco thought. *Kill this nigga for my brother's memory, then maybe, I can sleep better at night.* Fred wanted Sysco to stay in the car so they could peel off after he smoked this nigga, but Sysco wouldn't listen. They crept a few houses down, hoping the slob ass nigga left the same way he came. They watched as he picked up his bike and started walking toward them with his head down. Fred and Sysco ran from the side of the house with their guns aimed high. They heard someone yell and looked at the shorty on the porch, but it was too late...

DeWayne sat at the table and took the dope out of the bag. He remembered he needed more bullets and ran out of the house to catch Menace. Cliff opened the screen door and moved out of his way.

"Where's Menace?" DeWayne asked, rushing past him.

He saw Menace looking at his pager and then two niggas with guns jogging across the street towards him.

"Menace!" he yelled, his gun already raised and firing.

DeWayne hit one man in the chest, then shoulder, neck, and face before the man went down. The other man aimed his gun at DeWayne and got the first shot off before Cliff shot him six times in the mid-section.

When the shooting stopped, Carmelo stood and saw Cliff and DeWayne standing with their guns out.

"Put those guns up," he said, running toward them. "Y'all keep y'all heads down and go to Jamal's. Stay there until I get there!"

Carmelo looked around for witnesses and saw the fiend Jerry shot in the shoulder. Carmelo got on his bike and rode to Jenny's.

He ran into the house, put the Calico up, and got the keys to Jenny's car.

As Carmelo rode down 35th, he could hear police sirens coming from everywhere. *I have to get rid of those guns before the lil' niggas get booked.* He pulled in front of Jamal's house and knocked on the door.

"Where they at?" Carmelo asked.

Cliff and DeWayne appeared from behind the door.

"Where're the guns?"

"We got 'em," Cliff told him.

"Well, let's go."

They drove to the Mississippi River where Carmelo threw both guns.

"Where do you stay, Cliff?" Carmelo asked on their way back to Minneapolis.

"On 31st and Cedar."

"What about you?" he asked DeWayne.

"On 35th and Oakland."

"Tonight you'll stay at Cliff's. We need to let this shit die down," Carmelo said as they pulled in front of Cliff's building. "Y'all listen. If the police ever come looking for y'all, you know not to talk to them, right?"

"Yeah," Cliff said, and DeWayne nodded his head.

"If they ever take you downtown, DeWayne, what do you say?"

"I say, 'I don't want to talk to you,'" DeWayne told him.

"Cliff, what do you say?" Carmelo asked, looking at Cliff.

"I say, 'I ain't got nothing to say.'"

"Listen," Carmelo began, "after the police read you your rights, they ask you, 'Would you like to speak with us?' You tell them, 'I want a lawyer.' That's all you say. Say it one time so I can hear it, 'cause I don't want any excuses."

"I want a lawyer," Cliff and DeWayne said in unison.

"Today never happened. I don't want to hear about it anymore. Don't talk about it with nobody, not even each other. Cliff, give DeWayne something to wear and give me y'all clothes."

Carmelo went into the kitchen and found a bag to put their clothes in.

"Y'all stay in for the night, tomorrow is a new day. Stay away from the hood for a while, too," Carmelo told them before he left.

# Chapter 31

## Carmelo

Carmelo stayed away from the hood too. He hadn't talked to his mom in a while and decided to give her a call.

"Hey, Momma."

"Hey, boy. How are you doing?"

"I'm good, how about you?"

"I'm blessed, baby. Your momma just got a chance to run her own business!"

"What you do?"

"I got my daycare license, and my apartment just got approved."

"That's good, Momma. Do you have any kids lined up?"

"No. Just Stephen's."

"How much do you charge a month?"

"It's 65 dollars a week, so about 260 dollars a month."

"What are your hours?"

"Anytime. Why are you asking so many questions?"

"Because you are a godsend. I've been looking for a daycare to put my kids in."

"Crystal can bring Ciara. I'll watch her."

"What about J.R. and Colleen?"

"Who are they?"

"Those are my other two babies. You didn't hear me when I said kids?"

"Yeah, I did, but I didn't pay it no mind. You have three kids?"

"Yeah, Momma. I do."

"How old are they?"

"Two months."

"Both of them?"

"Three days apart."

"You are your daddy's son," she said and laughed.

"When can you start?"

"Whenever you want me to."

"Okay. Thank you, Momma."

"Anytime. I love you."

"I love you too, Momma," he said and hung up the phone.

Carmelo called Maria.

"Hello?"

"How are you doing?" Carmelo asked her.

"Who is this?" she demanded.

"It's Mike."

"What time is it?"

"It's 9:30 a.m."

"You're up this early?"

"Every day," Carmelo lowered his tone. "What are you doing?"

"I'm still in bed."

"You want me to call you back or come over and hold you while you sleep?" he asked, jokingly.

Maria was quiet for a while.

"Come over," she finally said and hung up.

Carmelo walked out the door with a pep in his step.

# Chapter 32

---

# Maria

Carmelo pressed the doorbell and waited. Seconds later, Maria opened the door in a robe.

"Lock the door."

Carmelo did as she asked and followed her to the bedroom. The room was dark, so he closed the door and found the bed. He took off his shirt and pants and laid down. Maria crawled over, put her head on his chest, her arm across his stomach, and fell asleep. Carmelo held her and closed his eyes.

When he opened his eyes, it was six after eleven, and Maria was snuggled close to him with her head on his shoulder and body pasted to the side of his. She wore a belly shirt, and he had his hand on her lower back, just above her ass. Her thigh was hung over his, and her hand had somehow gotten inside of his boxers lightly holding the base of his dick. His penis was erect, and he wondered how long it had been there.

Carmelo lightly scratched her lower back. She nuzzled closer. She moved her body over, so she was more on top of him and slid her hand deeper into his boxers. He laid there and thought to himself, *she can't be asleep.* After fifteen more minutes of lying there, he had to piss. He didn't want to, but he took her hand out of his boxers and went to use the bathroom.

Carmelo washed his hands and used a little bit of her mouthwash. When he returned to the bed, Maria went to the bathroom. She came back a couple of minutes later and straddled him.

"Did you sleep good?" Carmelo asked and put his hands on her hips.

"I don't think that I've ever slept better."

"Well, can I have my kiss now?"

Maria bent down and kissed him long and deep, then laid her head on his chest.

"I could stay like this all day."

"Do you want to?"

"Yes, but let's take a shower first," she told him and took his hand.

Maria turned the shower on and then turned toward him and raised her arms in the air. Carmelo raised the belly shirt over her head and laid it on the floor. He then hooked his thumbs into the sides of her panties and pulled them down. Maria stood in front of him naked.

She took a step toward him, put her hands inside of his boxers, and pulled them down. Their eyes explored each other's bodies before getting into the shower. When they were finished, they walked to the bedroom. Maria turned on the lamp, put her arms around Carmelo's neck, and kissed him.

Maria led Carmelo to the bed and laid him down. She kissed his mouth, his neck, working her way down. She sucked on his nipples and kissed his stomach. Maria removed his towel and admired his dick, as it stood long and hard at attention. She licked around the tip like it was an ice cream cone before taking him into her mouth. She sucked the head of his dick, sending sensations to Carmelo's toes. Then she sucked a little more, and a little more, until she had all she could take. Carmelo watched Maria as she took her time with him.

He'd had his dick sucked a lot, but it had never felt this good. He felt himself about to cum and stopped her. It was his turn.

He laid Maria on her back and rubbed his tongue across her neck. He kissed down to her breast, slowly licking around the areola before taking her nipple into his mouth. Carmelo made his way to her belly button, and then lower.

She was completely shaven and had a beautiful pussy. Carmelo gave her slow kisses from her pelvis to her clitoris. He lifted the skin above her pearl, revealing the pink bud, and rubbed his tongue across it.

"Oooh," she moaned and touched the top of his head.

He smiled to himself, Jenny had taught him well.

Carmelo lifted the skin a little more and began to lick and suck on Maria's clitoris as if it was a jolly rancher. He went lower and began licking around her outer lips and feasting on her pussy. Then he stuck his tongue in her.

"Ooh, Mike," she moaned, and he stopped.

He thought that he was tripping, then realized he was Mike to her and continued. Carmelo attacked her clit again and put his middle finger inside of her, causing her to spasm. He got on the bed and looked Maria in the eyes as he entered her.

"Aaah," she moaned as he filled her.

He started slow, in and out, until she arched her pelvis. Then he began to long stroke her. Maria brought her knees to her chest, giving him all of her.

"Harder . . . Harder . . ." she moaned, and Carmelo begin to pump into her hard and fast. "Fuck me Mike . . . Just like that," she told him as she matched him stroke for stroke. Maria had her second orgasm. Carmelo put her legs on his shoulders, causing them to almost touch her ear, and began pounding her.

"Shit . . . Fuck . . . Mike, stop . . . It hurts . . . Ooh . . . ooh . . . Mike. Ooh . . . Right there!" she moaned and climaxed a third time.

Carmelo had gotten into rhythm and knew he couldn't last much longer. He began to pump faster and go deeper. Carmelo came hard inside of Maria, emptying his nut sack. He let go of her legs and collapsed on top of her.

# Chapter 33

# Maria

Carmelo felt Maria's hand stroking his face and opened his eyes.

"Hi."

"Hi," he replied and turned toward her.

"Are you hungry?" she asked.

"Yeah."

They showered and he sat in his boxers and watched her in the kitchen.

"What do you want to eat?" She wore a pair of panties and another belly shirt.

"Besides you?"

She blushed and opened the freezer.

Carmelo got up, stood behind her, and wrapped his arms around her waist. She leaned her head back and put her hand over his.

"Fish sticks," he told her when he saw them in her freezer.

"Fish sticks?" she asked, surprised.

"Fish sticks." He reached for the box.

"Are you serious?"

"Yes, I am," he said with a serious face.

Maria snatched the box from him.

"I got it. Is this all you want to eat?"

"Macaroni and cheese, if you got any," he told her, and she shook her head.

They ate fish sticks with macaroni and cheese for brunch. Afterward, she walked up behind him and wrapped her arms around his waist.

"You have some place you have to be?" she asked, and he turned around to face her.

"I'm already here," he told her, and they kissed.

# Chapter 34

# Carmelo

A week later Carmelo rode his bike to Central Green's gym and walked in. He watched the five-on-five being played as he surveyed the gym. He saw his brother Stephen walking towards him.

"What's up, Stephen?"

"What's up, lil' bro?"

"Shit. Who got next?" he asked.

"We do. Have you talked to Momma?"

"Nah, why?"

"I guess the police came by the house asking about you."

"When?"

"Early this morning, I guess. She told me when I dropped Daphne off."

"Good looking."

He was about to leave the gym when he saw two police officers walk in holding a piece of paper. Carmelo observed them looking at the faces of individuals in the gym and put his head down. He began walking towards the other set of doors, hoping to make a quiet escape. Carmelo made the mistake of taking one last look towards the officers. They made eye contact, and it was the recognition in the officer's eyes that made Carmelo run.

The police gave chase, following him outside the gym. Carmelo saw a squad car in the parking lot and ran towards 35th and Clinton Avenue. He cut through townhomes, crossed 4th Avenue, cut through one yard, and then another. He ran across 5th Avenue, cut through the limousine rental lot, and through another yard.

Carmelo ran across Portland Avenue and looked back. When he didn't see any cops, he put his gun in the dumpster and walked through the alley towards 36th. When he got to the corner, a squad car was waiting for him. He turned to run in the opposite direction, but the two officers who started the chase were standing behind him with their guns drawn. *Damn, I'm out of shape*, he thought as he put his hands in the air.

# Chapter 35

# Detective Turner

"How do we approach this, James?" Richard Young, the Homicide Detective asked his partner. Detective Turner sat and pondered the situation.

Cliff and DeWayne were arrested earlier in the day and he knew they had to break one of them. Jerry wasn't going to be a good enough witness by himself. He had a long criminal record and wasn't reliable.

Detective Turner had two dead men and no witnesses other than a dope fiend. He had no gun, suspects but no confession, and with no confession, he'd have to let them go in thirty-six hours. This had been a hard year. They were already overloaded with unsolved murders and shootings and had to make a bust soon. Every day somebody was either getting shot or killed, and no one was talking.

Detective Turner grabbed the aspirin on his desk and downed three with a Coke.

"Let's go, Richard," he said to his partner as he got out of his chair.

Cliff sat in the bare room and stared at the wall. *How do the police know who I am and where I stay?* He never brought anyone to his house except DeWayne and Menace. He knew DeWayne didn't say anything; they had been together until they were arrested, and he was a hundred percent sure Menace knew how the game went. *But Menace was the one who told us to go to Jamal's house; he was the one who came and took us to throw the guns in the river. He was the one who told us—*

"Hi, Cliff," Detective Turner said, interrupting his thoughts. "My name is Sergeant James Turner, and this is my partner Sergeant Richard Young. We are Homicide Detectives and would like to ask you a couple of questions."

"I want a lawyer."

Detective Turner looked at his partner, then at Cliff. "What did you say, son?"

"I want a lawyer."

"We haven't even Mirandized you yet. You're not charged with anything, son. We're just going to ask you a few questions. Is that okay?" Detective Turner asked.

Cliff nodded his head.

"Good," he continued with a smile. "You want some water? Do you have to use the bathroom?"

"No," Cliff answered. "I just want a lawyer."

Detective Turner's face turned red, his blood pressure rose, and he broke the pencil in his hand. He wanted to beat the shit out of this kid; instead, he and Detective Young left the room.

# Chapter 36

# Detective Young

DeWayne paced the interrogation room, looking in the two-way mirror to see if anyone was back there, but it was too dark. He had to piss and wondered how long it was going to take them to come and talk to him.

He and Cliff met two girls last month and were supposed to be hooking up with them. *It's funny,* he thought, *how people notice you when you have money.* He was a virgin until he started selling dope for Menace. Now, fiends wanted to suck his dick and hoes wanted to fuck, and he was loving it. He was never going to be broke again. He wasn't hungry anymore at night; there were no more holes in his shoes, no more hand-me-down clothes, and he loved it.

*Damn! Where are these people at? I have to piss.*

"We have to find a different approach," Detective Turner told his partner. "If Cliff knew what to say, believe me, DeWayne will too. Carmelo taught them well. Fucking piece of shit nigger."

Detective Young was used to his partner using racial slurs. He felt the same way but never verbalized it. He wanted to be the chief of police one day.

"Let's treat him like a kid," Detective Young suggested. "Let me try something."

When they walked into the interrogation room, DeWayne was pacing. He stopped when the door opened and stared at them.

"I have to use the bathroom," DeWayne told the Detectives.

Detective Young walked DeWayne to the bathroom.

"What's up, DeWayne? How are you doing?" Detective Young asked, making small talk.

"I'm all right, tired of being in that little room."

"I know it's small, I'll get you out of there as soon as possible, I promise," Detective Young said as DeWayne went into the bathroom.

He stood by the door, then thought about another plan. He went to the vending machine and bought a Pepsi, Grandma Cookies, and a bag of Cheetos, and sat them on the table.

When DeWayne came out of the bathroom Detective Young motioned to him, and they walked back into the interrogation room.

"If you have to use it again, let me know," Detective Young told DeWayne in a friendly voice.

"Alright, thanks."

In the interrogation room, Detective Turner sat in the chair against the wall. He had brought in a desk chair for DeWayne to sit in and Detective Young closed the door.

"I brought you something to snack on," Detective Young told him, motioning to the food.

DeWayne opened the pop and Grandma cookies.

"How are you doing?" Detective Turner asked.

"Alright," DeWayne told him as he ate the cookie.

"You want to call your mom or dad?"

"Nah," DeWayne said. "I don't know my dad and my mom's not home."

"Well, we would like to ask you a few questions. Is that all right?"

"Yeah, that's cool," DeWayne said as he took a swallow of pop.

"Before we start, we have to read you your rights."

"Okay," DeWayne said, eating his other cookie.

"You have the right to remain silent . . ."

Detective Young watched DeWayne as Detective Turner recited the Miranda.

"Do you understand what I just said?"

"Yeah."

"Would you still like to talk to us?"

"No," DeWayne told the Detectives and took another swig of pop. "I would like a lawyer."

Detective Turner slammed his fist on the table, and Detective Young stared at DeWayne. He thought he had him. Detective Young became angry. He'd just been played by a thirteen-year-old kid. DeWayne looked at him, shrugged his shoulders, and finished his cookie. Detective Young grabbed the bag of Cheetos as he and Detective Turner left the room.

# Chapter 37

# Carmelo

Carmelo sat in the interrogation room and thought about Maria, his Maria. They had made love for three days, and it left him with mixed feelings. He hadn't felt this way since Crystal. Yeah, he loved Bunny and Jenny, but Crystal was his Queen. If he would have gotten a job, worked, and been a positive individual, he would have left Bunny and Jenny a long time ago, and been faithful to Crystal. He wasn't that fortunate, and because of that, knew he could never have her.

He told Maria as much as he could about himself. He lied about his kids, his name, and his age. *Are lies that small too big to forgive,* he thought as he stared at the wall.

He knew from the first moment he saw her that it was more than infatuation and lust. He made love to her not even twenty-four hours ago and now look at where he was. *I hope them lil' niggas were still laying low.*

When Detective Young opened the door, Carmelo was about to ask for his lawyer when he saw Cliff and DeWayne being led away in handcuffs. Detective Young closed the door and Carmelo closed his eyes.

Detectives Turner and Young were back at their desk. They had been duped twice by thirteen-year-old kids and knew that without a confession they would have to let the three of them go.

They knew Carmelo wasn't going to talk. He hadn't talked about the murder from last year he was rumored to have committed and knew this time would be no different and decided to try something new. If Carmelo saw Cliff and DeWayne, he might get nervous and talk. *I know he doesn't trust those kids*, Detective Young thought. So he had the boys brought out, and opened the door to Carmelo's interrogation room, faking a conversation, then shut the door. We'll give him another hour and let that brew.

An hour later, Detectives Turner and Young walked into the room. Carmelo had fallen asleep, so Detective Young touched his chair.

"Lawyer," Carmelo said and put his head back down.

The Detectives left, slamming the door as they did.

# Chapter 38

# Carmelo

Two days later, Carmelo saw Cliff and DeWayne. He had left Maria's and was driving down Lake Street when he spotted them at the bus stop.

"What's up, lil' niggas?" Carmelo asked as they got into the car.

"Shit," DeWayne said.

"What y'all doing at the bus stop at eleven in the morning?"

"We just came from some hoe's house," Cliff said proudly.

"Y'all got up this early to go get some pussy?" Carmelo asked.

"Nah, we spent the night," DeWayne told him.

"How old are the girls?"

"Fourteen," DeWayne answered.

"Where was their mom?"

"At the bar," Cliff told him.

Carmelo shook his head. "On a serious note, that was some real shit y'all did. You do that shit every time because if they had us, they wouldn't need to talk to us. I got y'all a place to move into on the first." Carmelo told them. "No bullshit at that house. It's in my name, so no loud music, no whores going in and out, and no booping out or around the house."

"This is a three-bedroom apartment, so you won't have to worry about somebody stealing from you, locking you out, or anything else."

Cliff and DeWayne smiled at one other.

"This is the last month y'all will work for me too, so save your money."

"Why?" Cliff asked, confused.

"Because you're old enough to buy your own goods and make your own money."

Carmelo's pager went off.

"Hello?" Chris said into the phone.

"What's up, nigga?"

"Where you at?"

"I'm at the pad. What's up?" Carmelo lied.

"Somebody just tried to kill Mark, thinking he was you."

"What?" Carmelo yelled into the phone as he sat up.

"Yeah, if C.J. wouldn't have shown up, they would have smoked him."

"Where's Mark at now?" Carmelo asked his brother.

"Right here."

"I'm at 3452 Blaisdell. Apartment 8. Bring him and come over," Carmelo said and hung the phone up.

Mark was Carmelo's first cousin twice. Their mothers were sisters and their fathers were brothers. They were a month apart and although they were cousins, they looked alike, Mark was just heavier. They had this joke where they would tell females that they were twin cousins.

Carmelo hit the buzzer and seconds later, Mark and Chris walked through the door.

"What happened?" Carmelo demanded when the door closed.

"I was on Chicago and Lake waiting at the bus stop when this car pulled up on me. Two niggas got out and rushed me. The nigga in the car had a gun pointed at me and said, 'What's up, Menace, you slob ass nigga.' I stood there at first 'cause I didn't know what the hell they were talking about. I told them that I wasn't 'Menace' and didn't know a nigga named Menace either. One of the niggas pulled out a gun, on Lake Street, and was about to shoot me, but C.J. showed up out of nowhere and stopped them. He told them that I was his cousin and wasn't in a gang and the niggas got in the car and left."

"Who were the niggas?" Carmelo asked his cousin.

"I don't know," Mark said. "But C.J. said they were Family Mob."

Carmelo sat there. *Why do these niggas think that I'm a Blood?* "You good now, nigga?" Carmelo asked his cousin.

"Yeah, I'm straight."

"Do you need anything?"

"Nah, I'm straight cousin, you be careful though. Them niggas weren't playing," Mark said with concern.

"You have a way to the pad?" Carmelo asked.

"Chris is going to take me."

Carmelo shook his head. He knew it was just a matter of time.

"You got your license?" Carmelo asked his little brother.

"Nope."

"But you got a car?"

"Yep."

Carmelo knew there was no point in talking to Chris further. His mind was on what happened tonight and the Family Mobs.

# Chapter 39

---

# Menace

Peavey Park was the hangout spot for the Bogus Boys, Family Mob, and Six-0 Crips. When Cliff pulled to the corner of Park and Franklin, he and Carmelo looked at all the niggas and bitches, fiends, and dope dealers in the park. Franklin had been a hot spot for a few years, making it possible for a nigga to make a thousand dollars a night if he wanted to.

The light turned green, and Cliff turned right onto Franklin. Carmelo waited until he saw the crowd of niggas he didn't like before raising the Tech .9 out the window and pulling the trigger. The niggas in the park ran toward Chicago, where Chris and DeWayne were lying in wait for them. Cliff turned on Columbus and then 18th. Making a left on Portland Avenue, he headed towards the hood.

"Drive normal," Carmelo told him as they got closer to Lake Street.

Cliff turned into Bunny's alley a few minutes later and stopped at her garage. Carmelo got out of the car with the Tech and watched Cliff drive down the alley.

Carmelo was backing his car out the garage when DeWayne pulled up. Chris put the AK47 in the trunk of Carmelo's car and was about to walk off when Carmelo stopped him.

"Drop them lil' niggas off at home Chris, and then take your ass home. Alright."

Chris's car was parked on 48th and 1st Avenue. "Alright, bro. I got you."

# Chapter 40

---

# Brian

"What's up, my nigga?" Brian asked when Carmelo called him back.

"Shit, just kicked back."

"What you getting into today?"

"I don't know yet, why? What's up?"

"We're about to have a little party over here."

"What you mean, party?" Carmelo asked, skeptically.

"A couple of lame friends are coming over. We're going to barbecue and play some games," Brian told him.

"What time?"

"I'm about to start the grill now."

"I'll stop through later."

"You know who is going to be there," Brian said in a playful voice.

He didn't know Carmelo and Maria were a couple.

"I'll stop through, Dog," Carmelo said, nonchalantly.

"Man, bring your ass through, I gotta holler at you." Brian hung up.

When Carmelo arrived at Brian's, he didn't see Maria's car.

"Hey, Mike," Melinda greeted him at the door.

"Hey, Melinda, how are you?"

"Fine," she answered. "You're here early."

"Yeah, I have to talk to Brian about something."

"He's out back playing with the grill," she told him, and Carmelo headed that way.

Lil Brian and Brianna were playing on the trampoline.

"Hey, Mike," they said, almost in unison.

"Hey, Brian, Brianna."

"You were always coming, weren't you?" Brian asked him.

"You're my nigga. If you need me to be at a deadass party with some lame-ass people, I'm here for you." They laughed.

Carmelo grabbed a Coke from the cooler and stood by the grill.

"I might have another lick in a few days," Brian told Carmelo as he turned the meat.

"Just let me know when, my nigga."

"So, how is everything going with you?"

Carmelo told him about his mom's daycare and spending time with his kids. He also told him about Chris and the shit he was doing.

"Sometimes you have to let them learn on their own. Once that money starts disappearing from the police taking his car or from the impound lot, he'll start to wisen up, trust me. That's why I did what I did for you because I had to learn the hard way."

The guests started showing up a little while later. Carmelo thought that it was going to be a small gathering of ten to twelve people at the most, but he was wrong. The backyard quickly became filled with people of all races.

"These are all Melinda and Maria's friends from high school and college. They're cool as hell, but I'm a nigga. I can't help it," Brian said as Maria walked out the backdoor.

"There she goes," he said and tapped Carmelo on the shoulder.

Carmelo turned around and saw Maria standing on the stairs. She wore a sundress and had her hair in a ponytail. *Man, she is beautiful.* Their eyes locked and if by instinct, they began walking towards one another.

"Where you going?" Brian asked, but Carmelo ignored him.

Maria skipped into his arms and they kissed.

"Hey, baby."

"Hey."

"You look lovely."

"Thanks," she said and did a 360-degree turn for him.

He took her hand and they walked back toward the grill.

"What's up, B?" Maria said to Brian.

"You tell me? You're the one kissing on my nigga. Got his nose wide open and shit."

Brian looked at Maria, then Carmelo, shook his head, and went back to grilling.

# Chapter 41

# Carmelo

Brian met Carmelo at the spot two days later. "What's up, lil' nigga?"

"Shit, just finishing this shit up." Carmelo was sitting in front of a table full of bagged-up dope. "I need a brick man, Dog," Carmelo said after a moment.

"What do you mean?" Brian asked, looking at the table.

"I mean, once this shit runs out, I'm gonna need to start copping on my own, and I don't want to buy nothing less than a brick."

"We should be hitting a lick next week that should keep you straight for a while."

"After that, I'm still gonna need a plug." Carmelo sat back and looked at Brian. "We're not going to be hitting a lick every week or once a month, Dog, so I'm gonna need a dude soon."

"We'll deal with that when we come to it. I promise," Brian said, ending the conversation.

◆ ◆ ◆ ◆

The next day Carmelo copped an eighth from Biz and called Chris.

"Hello."

"Where you at?" Carmelo asked his brother.

"I'm at the spot."

"Cool. I'm on my way."

Two things were wrong when he got there. Number one, Chris's car was parked outside. Number two, he saw his cousin Mark.

"What's up, nigga?" Carmelo asked Chris.

"Shit, what's up with you?" Chris asked when he saw the look on his brother's face.

"What's up, Melo?" Mark asked.

"Shit. What are you doing here?" Carmelo asked him.

"Chris asked if I wanted to make some money, and I told him yeah."

Carmelo looked from Mark to Chris.

Chris sat the safety pin down he was using to break the chunk of crack with and looked at his older brother. "That nigga's broke too, just like we were. Shit, that's my cousin, and I'm not gon' ever let him starve," Chris said with conviction.

His family had too many members and not enough money to go around. Carmelo let go of his anger.

"You know the rules, right?" Carmelo asked Mark.

"What rules?"

"Nigga, we don't talk to the police," Carmelo looked at Mark. "That rule, nigga."

"We already talked about that," Chris chimed in.

"Nigga, I ain't talking to you, we haven't talked about shit," Carmelo told his brother, then turned his attention back to Mark. "You know the rules, right?"

"Yeah, nigga, I do," Mark said. "I know to ask for a lawyer if the police ever catch me."

"Alright," Carmelo said. "And next time you try to do some shit without letting me know, I'm cutting you the fuck off. You don't run shit. I'm trying to help you out as best as I can because you're my brother, but I've been too nice to you. From now on, you listen to me, nigga or you do shit on your own. The object of the game is to not get caught. You're out here being flashy, driving flashy cars, and doing dumb shit and that's going to get you bumped, which might get me bumped, and if I get bumped over some stupid shit you did, I'm fucking you up."

Carmelo continued. "Now, put that fucking car up. Stop drawing attention to the spot and to yourself. Start thinking before you do shit, bro. I love you to death, nigga, but I got too many mouths to feed to let anybody fuck this shit up for me. Understand?"

Chris stared at Carmelo for a few seconds before answering.

"Yeah, nigga," Chris said.

"Here." Carmelo sat the dope on the table. "Here's four and a half. Call me when you need more."

# Chapter 42

---

# Jamal

Carmelo was riding his bike heading towards Central Park when he saw Jamal.

"What's up, lil' nigga?" he asked.

"Shit, just riding through the hood," Jamal told him. "What you up to?"

"Nothing, just trying to get these goods off."

"I know a spot where there's a lot of fiends."

"Where?" Carmelo asked, curiously.

"Come on, follow me." Jamal took him to a house on 38th and Oakland.

"What's up, Cousin Greg?" Jamal said to the man who opened the door.

"Hey, Jamal, what's up?" he said, eyeballing Carmelo.

"I'm good. This is J.J.'s friend, Menace."

Carmelo gave him a head nod.

"He's looking for a spot to set up shop in."

"You got work?" Cousin Greg asked.

"Yeah."

Cousin Greg looked at Jamal. "You say he's J.J.'s friend?"

"Yeah. He was always around the house. He was one of the pallbearers."

"I can't remember. I was too fucked up over his death." Cousin Greg was quiet for a minute and then he looked at Carmelo. "I need a forty a day."

"Cool."

Cousin Greg let them in the house and disappeared into the kitchen.

"Who's Cousin Greg?" Carmelo asked. "I don't remember him."

"He used to be married to my cousin. They were together before I was born. She used to smoke too but stopped a few years ago. He couldn't, so she left him."

"Is he cool?"

"Yeah. He keeps a job and pays his bills. He just smokes up the rest. Cousin Greg is cool. He doesn't steal or be on that funny shit."

Carmelo sat down and put two pills on the table.

"It's slow right now, but watch when it gets dark," Jamal told Carmelo. Cousin Greg came out of the kitchen and stared at the pills on the table. "Are those for me?"

"Yeah," Carmelo said.

Greg picked up the pills and left.

The day went by slow, but true to his word, the darker it got, the busier it became. Carmelo observed the relationship Jamal had with the fiends and how comfortable he was at Cousin Greg's.

By one that morning, Carmelo was out of goods and Jamal was asleep on the couch.

"Wake up, lil' nigga. Let's go."

Carmelo dropped Jamal off at his house and gave him two hundred dollars.

"What's this for?" he asked, surprised.

"For looking out."

Carmelo went to Bunny's to grab some more dope and headed out the door without saying a word. She knew the game, it was grind time.

# Chapter 43

---

# Jamal

Later that morning Jamal showed up.

"What's up, Menace?"

"Shit. What are you doing up so early?"

"Came to kick it with you."

"You know how to boop?" Carmelo asked.

Jamal gave him a sour look. "Are you serious? I used to be here with my older brother when I was twelve years old," he said with pride.

"How old are you now?"

"I'll be fourteen next month."

Carmelo lit a cigarette and eyed Jamal. "Have you ever been locked up?" Carmelo asked him, seriously.

"I've been to JDC a few times, but they had to let me go."

"Why?"

"Because they ain't have shit, and I ain't tell 'em shit."

"That's real, lil' nigga."

"Yeah. J.J. and my brother taught me the game. I know not to talk to the police."

"You want to sell this shit while I run to SA?" Carmelo asked him. He was hungry and had to get something in his stomach.

"Yeah, I'll do it," Jamal said.

Carmelo handed him enough dope to hold him and went to Cup on 38th and Chicago Avenue.

Carmelo thought about J.J. He was a good nigga, a stand-up nigga. More like a brother to Carmelo than his own. When he died, Carmelo had no choice but to retaliate. They killed his best friend, what else was he supposed to do. Carmelo saw a lot of J.J. in Jamal and that made him feel good.

Brian paged him an hour later.

"Hello?"

"What's up, my nigga."

Shit. What's going on?" Carmelo asked.

"It's all good, my nigga. Meet me at the spot."

Carmelo understood what that meant and got up to leave.

"Jamal, I have to go for a few hours. Can you hold me down?"

"I got this," Jamal told him, and Carmelo handed him the bag of goods.

Carmelo pulled the nine shot .45 from his waist. "Keep this with you at all times."

"I'm good, my nigga."

Jamal showed Carmelo the Smith and Wesson .9mm he had under his shirt. Carmelo nodded and walked out the door.

# Chapter 44

# Brian

Carmelo walked into the apartment in Northeast and saw Brian sitting on the couch eating a slice of pizza.

"What's up, my Nigga?" he asked.

"Busy."

"Busy?"

"Yeah, busy. I'm booping at this new spot with J.J.'s lil' relative Jamal, and I got Cliff and DeWayne at another spot."

"You don't want to do this?" Brian questioned.

"Nigga, if you can find a nigga every night that's going to give me a hundred thousand for free, I would leave my momma in the hospital bed, 'cause I know that it'll benefit her. So, I ain't complaining, my nigga."

"The nigga is an OG Shotgun Crip that sells a lot of drugs. He owns a studio, restaurants, and real estate, but he be supplying a lot of niggas with goods. Tanya said he's got his nephew working for him. She used to fuck with the nigga, but he cut her off last month, so she's pissed. All we have to do is wait until it's dark, catch the nephew leaving the house, and it's on from there. No bullshit, no hesitation."

Brian and Carmelo stood on the side of the house for the better part of thirty minutes before they heard the door open and shut. They pulled the masks down and watched as a fat nigga with a bag walked toward the two cars parked in the driveway.

Brian crept behind him and pointed the Smith and Wesson revolver at his midsection. "Give me that bag, you fat muthafucka."

When the man saw the revolver, he handed Brian the bag without saying a word.

"Come on," Brian told him.

Carmelo had the Glock in his hand as they walked up the stairs and tried the door. Brian knocked and waited until the door opened.

"Step back," he told the man he knew as Big Mike.

Big Mike looked from his nephew to the men with the guns in their hands and stepped back into the house.

"Sit your fat ass down," Brian told Big Mike when they got into the house. "You too, nigga. Find a seat."

Carmelo waited until Brian put the handcuffs on Big Mike and his nephew before he closed the windows and shades.

"I know that y'all are going to make this hard," Brian began. "So, before I even ask you where the shit is, let me show you how serious I am."

He pulled the .22 out of his pocket and handed it to Carmelo. "If neither one of these niggas speak up about where the shit is in the next ten seconds, kill him." Brian pointed at Big Mike's nephew.

"Ten . . . nine . . . eight . . . seven . . ." he started counting.

"Uncle Mike, give him the muthafuckin' money."

"Six . . . five . . . four . . . three . . ."

"Alright! Alright!" Big Mike yelled. "Untie me, so I can give you the money. It's in my safe."

"What's the combination?"

"I don't want to say it out loud. Untie me and I'll get the money for you. I promise," Big Mike said in a calmer voice.

"Are you willing to risk your nephew's life for some paper you can get again? You sell kilos of dope and own a lot of shit. You can always get the money back we're going to take today. The question is, does anybody have to die because of it?"

The house was quiet for a while.

"Two . . . one."

"Alright! Alright!" Big Mike yelled.

He gave Brian the combination to the safe. He opened it and saw the .38 snub-nosed revolver. *Slick muthafucka*, he thought, as he put the money in the bag.

When he got downstairs, he sat the bag down and looked at Big Mike.

"Now, the dope."

"I ain't got no dope," Big Mike protested, and Brian punched him square in the mouth.

Brian went into the small bag he brings on every robbery and pulled out some braided rope. He tied Big Mike's ankles to the chair and then balled up a tablecloth from the table and put it in Big Mike's mouth. He took the hammer out of the bag and stood in front of Big Mike.

"I see that you don't care about your nephew's life. Let's see how much you cherish your own." Brian swung the hammer and hit Big Mike directly in the center of his knee.

Big Mike's leg jerked, but it was tied to the chair, and did him no good. The noise Big Mike made through the cloth told of the pain he felt. The piss and tears ran as Brian looked at his other knee.

"Are you going to tell me where the dope is?" he asked and Big Mike nodded his head.

When the tablecloth came off of Big Mike's mouth, he threw up everything he had inside of him before telling Brian where the dope was.

Brian put the dope in the bag with the money and they walked out the door, leaving Big Mike and his nephew handcuffed.

# Chapter 45

# Carmelo

Carmelo pulled in front of Cousin Greg's early in the morning and walked into the house.

"It just slowed down about thirty minutes ago," Cousin Greg told him. He was sitting in a chair smoking a cigarette.

Carmelo walked over to Jamal who was sleeping on the couch, and tapped him. Jamal reached for his gun before he opened his eyes.

"It's me, lil' nigga," Carmelo told him. "Are you ready to go?"

Jamal's eyes were bloodshot red, and he looked exhausted. "I'm good."

"Come on, I'll drop you off at home. Tomorrow is a new day."

♦ ♦ ♦ ♦

Carmelo was at Bunny's house dropping off money and grabbing dope when he saw her pulling up. Bunny got out of the car and kissed him.

"Hey, baby, how are you doing?" he asked her.

"Tired. I just dropped your son off at your mom's," she said, looking irritated.

"What's wrong?" Carmelo asked her.

"This! This is what's wrong!" Bunny began to cry. "This is the extent of our relationship and has been for the past month."

"I'm sorry. It's going to get better real soon. I promise," he told her.

"Okay," Bunny wiped her eyes.

"I'll be home tonight to give you some of this dick," he told her, and she smiled. "I gotta take care of something, but tonight you get a booty call."

"I love you."

"I love you, too." Carmelo kissed her on the lips and got into his car.

# Chapter 46

---

# Brian

A few minutes later, Brian paged.

"What's up, my nigga?" Brian asked.

"Shit, taking care of business real quick. Give me an hour and I'll be there."

"All right, cool," Brian said and hung up.

An hour later, Carmelo walked through the door and wasn't surprised to see a Whopper in Brian's hands.

"What's up, my nigga?" he said as Carmelo closed the door.

"I'm good. Gotta go fuck my baby mommas tonight," he said, and Brian looked at him.

"Is that a bad thing?"

"Hell nah, but since I've been booping, I haven't been fucking that much. I'm not where I can take breaks yet," Carmelo said honestly.

"Don't speak too fast," Brian said and stood up.

They went into the dining room where Carmelo saw the table full of money.

"There were three hundred and thirty thousand dollars," Brian told him. "You get a hundred of that and I get the rest."

Brian always looked into Carmelo's eyes for a speck of anger or jealousy over getting less money, but never saw it. That's why he loved him and didn't mind giving him all the dope.

"You can use the bag on the floor right there," Brian told him.

Carmelo picked it up and looked at Brian.

"There are thirteen bricks in there," he told Carmelo, who nodded his head. "That should last you for a while."

"Yeah, it should," Carmelo said as he put the money in the bag with the dope.

"Maria's in love with you," Brian told him as they walked out of the door.

"How do you know?" Carmelo asked, looking Brian in the eye.

"Melinda told me."

Carmelo took a deep breath.

"I wonder if she'll still love me when she finds out my name isn't Mike, I have three kids, and I'm only seventeen."

Brian put his hand on Carmelo's shoulder.

"When you do tell her," Brian grinned, "make sure you tell her over the phone. She's a kickboxer."

Carmelo shook his head and got into his car.

# Chapter 47

# Crystal

Three days later Carmelo drove to Crystal's house with a lot on his mind. He had thirteen kilos of dope and could do what he wanted to. He knew niggas in the hood who'd been selling dope since he was a kid who probably hadn't seen half of that.

He had forty thousand at Jenny's and decided to give Crystal and Bunny fifty thousand a piece to put up.

"Hey, baby," Crystal said and kissed him.

He walked into the apartment and closed the door.

"Hey, where's your mom?"

"At work," Crystal told him. "Ain't nothing changed."

They walked into her room and Carmelo looked at all the bags on the floor.

"What you get?" he asked.

"Some stuff for Ciara. Clothes, toys, formula, diapers, things she needs."

"What did you get for you?"

"I bought some panties and bras," she said and sat on the bed.

Carmelo sat next to her and opened the bag he brought with him.

"There's fifty thousand in here," he told her. "Don't ask no questions either, 'cause it doesn't matter. Put forty-five up and do not touch it without asking me. I mean it." He looked at her and she nodded. "The other five I want you to spend on you. If Ciara needs anything, I'll buy it, this is for you."

Carmelo counted out five thousand and set it on the bed.

"I mean it. That's for you to spend."

"I miss this, Carmelo," she said with a smile.

"I've missed you," he told her.

Carmelo kissed her, and Crystal wrapped her arms around him. She was rubbing her hands up and down his back when she felt the butt of the gun and pulled her face back.

"What's that?" she asked, and Carmelo pulled the gun from his waist.

"Carmelo, what are you doing out there?"

"I'm making sure that my baby doesn't grow up in a fucked up lower-class neighborhood, where muthafuckas don't pimp hoes in the daytime and kill niggas at night. I'm making sure my baby momma doesn't have to struggle taking care of my seed if anything happens to me. That's what I'm doing," he said, setting the gun on the dresser.

"Do you think that carrying a gun makes you a man?"

"Nah, carrying a gun makes sure I live to see my son grow up to be a man and my daughters' women," Carmelo snapped.

"Life was so much better a while ago, before you started selling dope. We were so much happier," she cried.

"No, you were so much happier. Your mom's a nurse and your brothers and sisters are grown, so you get whatever the fuck you want. I grew up in a house where my mom loved my brother more than she loved me. She bought him Nikes and Girbauds and I got XJ900s and Lee jeans. Only to move into a house where I sometimes didn't even exist. Where my brothers and sisters ate before me, and I got leftovers and hand-me-downs. So don't talk to me about better or happy. All I've had my whole life was me. You don't know how it feels to go a whole fucking day without eating or having to sleep outside because nobody would come open the door for you at night. To ball up and cry because you're sleeping in the garage with the dog, and he's got a bowl of food and water and you ain't got shit."

She sat stoically, listening to his heartbreaking words.

"So, don't ever talk to me about something being better or somebody being happy. I'm better now because I can supply for myself and my family. I'm happier 'because I got a place to stay, food in my mouth, clothes on my back, and I make sure my family has the same. And I'm gonna keep carrying this muthafuckin' gun and selling dope until I have no doubt my kids are set for life or until these muthafuckas kill me."

Carmelo put his gun on his waist and left Crystal crying on the bed.

# Chapter 48

# Carmelo

It was the middle of October when Carmelo decided to pick Carl up from school. He was parked out front, playing music when school was dismissed.

"Hi Carmelo," some of the females he knew greeted him.

Some of the Blood homies came across the street and shook his hand as Carl got into the car. He was about to pull off when he saw Nena. Nena was a petite female, caramel complexion, pretty with long black hair, small titties, and a tight ass. She grew up in the neighborhood and her entire family was Bloods. Nena decided to go to school instead of gang bang. Carmelo never tried to holler at her because Bunny was always around, but Bunny had graduated.

"What's up, girl?" he asked.

"Hi Carmelo," she said from across the street.

"Come over here."

"I'm gonna miss my school bus, then what am I gonna do?"

"Hop in the truck and let me take you home," he flirted with her.

She thought about it and then walked across the street and got in.

"What's up, Carl?"

"Hey, Nena, what's up?" Carl replied before he was drowned out by the music.

Jenny was at work, so Carmelo dropped Carl off, and Nena got in the front seat.

"So, how have you been?" Carmelo asked as he pulled off.

"Fine," she said in a shy voice.

"You're a senior now. The Queen Bee of Roosevelt," he said, and she laughed. "Who you looking good for?"

"How's Bunny?" she asked and threw him off.

"She's good, I guess. She lets me see my son whenever I want to, so we're good," he told her, knowing he had her.

"So, you and her aren't together?"

"Not for the last four months. I guess I'm too busy for her."

"That's sad. Y'all made a cute couple."

"Who you making a cute couple with these days?"

"Nobody. It seems like everybody's scared to talk to me or something."

"Nah, they know who your family is, and they're intimidated."

"Don't you like having such overprotective family members?" she said sarcastically and shook her head.

"I don't care who you're related to. I wouldn't let nobody stop me."

"From what?" she asked, feigning innocence.

"From talking to a girl I like. Especially if she looked like you."

They were at a stoplight and he was looking at her.

"You're bad," she said, blushing.

"I'm honest. I'd take the risk," he said, and she looked at him for a moment, contemplating.

"So, if I said, 'Carmelo, when you take me home, come inside and make love to me,' you'd come?" she asked as they stopped at another red light.

"Ask me," he dared her, looking seductively into her eyes. "And not only will I cum, I'll make sure you have an exploding orgasm, too."

They were quiet the rest of the way. Carmelo stopped in front of her house and put the truck in park, but kept the engine running. She sat there for a moment, looking straight ahead.

"Carmelo . . ."

"Yeah."

"Come inside."

He faced her. "Why?"

Nena turned and faced him. "To make love to me," she said and got out of the truck.

Carmelo wasn't far behind.

# Chapter 49

---

# Carmelo

In October, Bunny was pregnant again. In November, Nena was pregnant, and for Christmas, he found out Maria was pregnant.

It was the end of March when he heard from Crystal. They hadn't talked since the argument and he didn't want to call her back, but she had his daughter.

"Hello?"

He heard her voice and got angry all over again. "What's up?"

"How you doing, Carmelo?"

"Why'd you page me, Crystal? Is my daughter okay? Do you need something?"

She was silent for a moment.

"Your daughter has a doctor's appointment tomorrow. I have to work and can't take the day off, neither can my mom. Your mom can't leave the daycare either, so can you take her?"

"Hold on, I'm your last option?"

"I didn't know if you'd be busy or not."

"For my daughter?" he snapped. "You think my daughter doesn't come first in my life?"

"I don't know. The way you made it sound the last time we talked, the money came first," she snapped back.

"Crystal, you're going to make me say something real disrespectful to you."

"Say it," she dared, but Carmelo bit his tongue. He reached into his pocket for a cigarette and lit it. "What time is her appointment?"

"Noon."

"I'll pick her up from my mom's house."

# Chapter 50

---

# Carmella

The next day, Carmelo took his daughter to the hospital. When he walked into the waiting room, he saw Tiny, a girl he knew from the block, sitting with a little girl on her lap.

"Hey, Carmelo," she said as he sat down.

"What's up, Tiny?"

"What's up? What are you doing here?"

"My daughter has a doctor's appointment. You?"

"My grandma is sick. She had a heart attack about an hour ago and was rushed here."

Ciara wanted to get out of his lap, so Carmelo let her down and took her coat off. She'd been walking the last two months and it seemed like that's all she wanted to do.

"That's your daughter?"

"Yeah, that's my baby," he said with pride.

"What's her name?"

"Ciara. She'll be one, April fourth."

"She's a little cutie."

"She takes after her dad," he said and smiled.

He looked at the little girl balled up in Tiny's lap.

"How old is she?" Carmelo asked.

"Four."

The girl stirred and the way she slept reminded him of his own kids. Ciara tapped his knee and he looked into her smiling face.

"Dada," she said and raised her arms. Carmelo reached down and picked her up.

"Aah, she's so cute," Tiny said.

Carmelo looked at the baby Tiny was holding and saw her open her eyes and rub them. He used to love watching Ciara and Colleen do that. It looked so cute.

"What's up, my nigga?" Brian said as he walked in. "How's she doing?"

Carmelo was about to answer when Tiny spoke.

"They still have her in there. She's stable, but she's in a coma."

Brian walked over to the window and looked out. Carmelo watched him for a minute, then Tiny as she got up and took the little girl to the restroom. Brian sat in her place.

"That's your grandma in there, Dog?" Carmelo asked.

"Yeah," he answered.

Ciara started jumping up and down on his lap.

"Dada, let me down," she demanded, and Carmelo sat her on the floor.

Brian looked at him. "What are you doing here?" he asked, confused.

"My daughters got a doctor's appointment."

"Which one is she?" Brian asked, looking at Ciara.

"That's my oldest, Ciara."

They watched her by the window looking out onto the street. They'd been friends for about a year now and it was crazy how little they knew about each other. It was strictly business it seemed.

Tanya walked in a short time later.

"How's she doing?" Tanya asked Brian.

"We don't know yet," he told her, and she sat down next to him. She looked at Carmelo, who was watching his daughter look out the window.

"Hi Menace," she said sarcastically. "You can't speak?"

*She hasn't said two words to me since we first met and now, she's speaking to me?* He was wearing a pair of Rockport boots, a Polo outfit, and a thousand-dollar leather coat. He realized that was what she saw.

"What's up?" he replied and focused his attention on his daughter.

Tiny came back from the bathroom and sat on the opposite side of Tanya. Carmelo got Ciara from the window and held her hands as she stood between his legs. Tiny, Tanya, and Brian were talking, and Carmelo caught the little girl in Tiny's lap staring at him. He waited until there was a pause in their conversation before he spoke.

"Is she your daughter, Tiny?" he asked.

Brian stood and walked back to the window.

"Nah," Tiny said.

Carmelo tickled his daughter and looked at the girl across from him. He smiled at her and she smiled back.

"Hi, Carmella," Tanya said to the little girl.

Carmelo didn't hear anything else. He'd seen that smile every time he looked at his daughters and his son, and every time he looked in the mirror. It was his smile and somehow this girl was his daughter.

"Who's her mom?" he asked Tiny.

She looked at him strangely. "My cousin."

"What's her name?"

"Why?" Tiny asked, but Carmelo ignored the question.

"Do you know who her dad is?" he pressed, looking at the little girl.

"Why are you asking all these damn questions?" Tanya jumped in.

"Look at her," Carmelo said in an accusing tone. "Then look at my daughter."

Tiny and Tanya both looked.

"And?" Tanya asked, sarcastically.

"You don't see it, do you?" Carmelo asked. He was getting angry and frustrated. It was clear as day. "She's got my name."

"No, she doesn't," Tanya said.

"What does that mean?" Tiny said in an angry tone.

"Who's her mom?" he was mad now.

"I'm not telling you," Tanya said and stood up.

"What the fuck y'all arguing about?" Brian demanded.

"He's saying Carmella is his daughter," Tanya said, and Brian looked at him.

"Dog, what's her mom's name?" Carmelo asked one last time.

Before Brian could answer, they all heard a female's voice.

"Oh my God!"

# Chapter 51

# Brandy

Brandy was a thirteen-year-old virgin when she started hanging out with her cousins Sherry and Shalenda. Sherry was going with a guy named Chris and Shalenda was going with his cousin, Mark. Chris had an older brother named Carmelo. When Brandy saw Carmelo, she instantly liked him. He was cute and funny and two weeks later they played truth and dare, without truth. Brandy dared her cousin Sherry to have sex with Chris and Sherry accepted the challenge. Sherry in return dared Brandy to have sex with Carmelo. She liked him a lot and had to lose her virginity one day. *Why not lose it to someone I like,* she thought.

They walked into Sherry's room and Brandy turned out the lights.

"Why'd you turn out the lights?" Carmelo asked.

"Because I don't want you to see me naked," she said, and Carmelo laughed. "Do you have a condom?"

"Yeah, I do."

"Okay."

Brandy took off her clothes and sat on the edge of the bed. Carmelo joined her seconds later and touched her arm.

"You sure you want to do this?"

Brandy took a deep breath. "Yeah, I'm sure. Nigga, I ain't scared of you."

Carmelo laughed and grabbed her hand. "You don't have to be afraid of me. I'm not going to hurt you. But I can't vouch for him," Carmelo wrapped her hand around his swollen penis and Brandy gasped.

She was a virgin and hadn't seen or felt a dick before and didn't know what was considered big or average. All she knew was the feel of Carmelo's penis in her hand had her both scared and excited. So many different feelings and emotions were going through her.

"Lie back," Carmelo told her.

Brandy did as she was asked, her heart beating a mile a minute. Carmelo was gentle with her. He sucked on her neck and then her titties, sending vibrations through her body. Carmelo's hand traveled down her belly to her vagina. Brandy stopped him.

"We can stop if you want to," Carmelo told her.

Brandy thought about how she dared her cousin to have sex, and she didn't punk out and how bad she would feel if she and Carmelo didn't do it. Then she thought about how comfortable and patient Carmelo was with her.

*He has to be experienced*, she thought because he was not overbearing or demanding.

"No, I'm ready," Brandy said, releasing her grip on Carmelo.

Carmelo began playing with Brandy's vagina, and she found herself making sounds she only heard on television. He had her body feeling like nothing she's ever felt before, and she never wanted that feeling to end.

Carmelo got on top of her, and Brandy heard the condom wrapper being opened. Seconds later, Carmelo guided his penis into her. Brandy bit Carmelo on his shoulder.

"Ahh."

"I'm sorry. I'm sorry," she told him.

Carmelo took his time with her. He went in and out of her slow and then fast. He tried to put her legs in the air, but she wasn't ready for that. Her first orgasm took everything out of her. It felt like her soul was snatched. Her body convulsed and she became weak. Carmelo continued to pump into her, bringing her to another moment of ecstasy. Then it was over. Carmelo got off of her and began getting dressed.

"Are you good?"

"Yes. I'm good," she told him.

"Cool. I have to go," he told her. "Get dressed. I'll close the door when I leave."

Brandy watched Carmelo walk out the door and knew she loved him. What she didn't know was that the condom broke. A few weeks later when she started having morning sickness, she thought she had the flu. Her cousin Tanya took her to the hospital and the doctor told her she was pregnant.

Brandy was scared. If her cousin found out, he would kill Carmelo. Tanya told her she would support her either way, no matter her decision. Brandy was in love with Carmelo but was too scared to tell him. She didn't know how he would react. She told Tanya she wanted to keep the baby. Her and Carmelo's baby. This way she'd always have a piece of him. She swore Tanya to secrecy, so Brian never knew the baby's father's name. Brandy named her daughter Carmella and promised she'd tell Carmelo one day, and then they'd get married and live together forever. That's been her dream since she found out she was pregnant. One day, she kept telling herself. One day. Then she turned into the waiting room . . .

# Chapter 52

## Carmelo

"Brandy?" Carmelo asked.

"Hey, Momma," Carmella said and ran into her mother's arms.

Brandy bent down and hugged her daughter, keeping her eyes on Carmelo.

"Hi Carmelo," she said.

Carmelo took a few steps toward her. "Brandy, is this my daughter?"

The entire room was quiet. Everyone focused on Brandy, waiting for an answer.

"Yes, Carmelo. She is your daughter."

Carmelo walked to the nearest chair and sat down. He was shaking. He had a four-year-old daughter he never knew existed. He missed her first four birthdays and Christmases. He missed her first steps, her first words. He wondered if his daughter ever thought about him or missed him. He knew she was his daughter, and she obviously knew him too. *She knows me too*, he thought, and a tear rolled down his cheeks. She knew him at first sight.

He turned and looked at Carmella and saw her staring at him.

"Can I hold her?" he asked no one in particular.

"Yes," Brandy said and walked Carmella to him.

When they stood in front of him, Carmelo squatted down.

"Carmella," she said with tears in her eyes, "this is your dad."

Carmelo hugged his daughter, oblivious of Maria and Melinda, as they turned the corner.

# Chapter 53

# Maria

Maria saw Michael hugging Carmella, Tanya and Tiny in tears, and Brian with a smile on his face. She knew something happened; she just didn't know what. She saw the little girl who was a spitting image of Carmelo staring at her. Maria had seen those eyes before and when the girl gave her that crooked smile, she knew.

"Mike, what's going on?" she asked.

Carmelo heard Maria's voice and shook his head. *This has got to be the best as well as the worst day ever. How can God give me something so precious and take something so dear to me away at the same time?* He looked up.

"Mike, what's going on?" Maria asked again.

"Who is Mike?" Tanya asked, confused.

Carmelo stood and looked at Maria. Her eyes were watery.

"Baby, let's go somewhere and talk," Carmelo said to Maria.

"No! What is going on and what does she mean, 'who is Mike?'" Maria questioned.

"DaDa!" Ciara said, standing on the side of Carmelo. "Pick me up."

Maria took a step back and sat down.

Carmelo picked up Ciara and took a step towards Maria. The way she looked at him, made him stop.

"Is this your daughter?" she asked.

"Yes."

"So, you do have kids?"

"Yes."

"Is she your only one?"

"No."

"How many?"

"Four," he told her.

Maria gasped. "So, you lied to me?" Tears rolled down her cheeks.

"Yes."

"Is your name really Mike?" she asked, sarcastically.

"No."

"What's your name?" she asked, with unbelief on her face.

"Carmelo. Carmelo Graham."

"So, you lied to me?" she asked again, and Carmelo saw the hurt on her face. "Did you ever love me?"

"More than you know," he told her, but she wasn't listening.

"Or did you just want to fuck me?" Tears were pouring down her face.

"Maria, calm down, breathe. Let's go somewhere and talk."

"Graham?" the receptionist said. "The doctor is waiting."

Carmelo looked behind him at the receptionist and nodded his head. He then faced Maria.

"I have to take my daughter to see the doctor. Can we talk when I get back?"

"I don't ever want to talk to you again," Maria said and put her head in her hands.

Carmelo looked at her one last time, then turned around, and walked away. He stopped and hugged Carmella, and then carried Ciara towards the door.

# Chapter 54

## Chaos

veryone was lost in their own thoughts.

    Brian watched the situation unfold. He had never seen no shit like that before in his life. *That was some soap opera, Young and The Restless shit.* He'd never seen somebody get blessed and cursed in the same minute.

    Tanya sat there with so much on her mind. *Carmella's dad is Brian's stick-up partner?* Her heart went out to him. *This was probably the best, fucked up day of his life.* She remembered how Brandy would spend hours talking about him. She didn't know that he was fucking that stuck up bitch Maria either. That was interesting. *This young nigga might have some potential after all. Both of these bitches were obsessed with him. He probably knows how to fuck good,* she thought.

◆ ◆ ◆ ◆

Brandy saw him hug his daughter and knew her dream was going to come true. She and Carmelo would be together. Then Maria's stuck up ass came and spoiled everything, *or did she?* Maybe it was a good thing she came in when she did, now Carmelo wouldn't have any distractions. There were no more secrets and now that he knew Carmella was his daughter, she had a chance. She was going to make the best of it.

◆ ◆ ◆ ◆

Melinda watched the scene and couldn't believe her ears. She liked Mike, or Carmelo, whoever the fuck he was. He made her sister happy and that meant a lot to her. Brian had brought him to the house. She and Brian had conspired to set them up. Brian had brought Mike into their lives. Which means he knew that Mike was Carmelo and not Mike. He had a lot of explaining to do.

◆ ◆ ◆ ◆

*Why? He could have told me. He could have told me anything. I gave my heart to him, and he lied to me. Why? What reason would he have to lie about his name and his kids? Did he want to protect me from something? There's no excuse and I'm not going to make any for him either. I'm going to raise this baby on my own,* Maria thought.

# Chapter 55

---

# Carmelo

When Carmelo and Ciara finished seeing the doctor, the waiting room was empty. His head was spinning as he drove to Crystal's apartment. *Brandy knew who he was and could have found him. Chris still saw Sherry and Brandy lived with them. Why did she keep his daughter a secret?*

He'd seen Sherry and Shalenda multiple times since he and Brandy had sex and they never said anything. *Brandy better be lucky she was B-Dog's cousin, or she'd be a dead bitch.* He still couldn't get his daughter's face out of his head, or Maria's. He knew Maria would never forgive him.

He took Ciara home and then drove to his mom's apartment. Carmelo did something he hadn't done in years. He went to his old room, crawled into bed, and went to sleep.

When he opened his eyes, it was dark outside. He got up and walked into the living room.

"Hey, sleepyhead," his mom looked up from the television.

"Hey, Momma."

His dad was in the kitchen doing a crossword puzzle. Carmelo sat down on the couch.

"What happened? You looked drained when you walked through the door. You're not sick, are you?" she asked with concern.

"Nah, Momma."

"Did something happen?"

"Yeah. I found out I have a four-year-old daughter."

"What!" His momma yelled and his dad put his pen down.

Carmelo told them the whole story. When he was done, his dad shook his head and giggled.

"Boy, you got the worst luck in the world," he said as his mom shushed him.

"Don't pay attention to him. Your dad's silly. How are you doing?" she asked in her motherly tone.

"I'm emotionally drained. I am. I love Crystal so much, but I had to cut her off because she didn't feel my struggle. Maria took her place and now I lost the two best things that happened to me so far," he told her, and his dad interjected.

"You said it right, boy, 'so far.' Don't let them girls mess your head up. Too many of 'em out there. Keep doing what you're doing. As long as you're taking care of them kids and taking care of home, the hell with everybody else and what they think and how they feel."

They sat there in silence for a moment.

"So, when do we get to meet her?" his mom finally asked.

"I'll bring her by on Ciara's birthday," he said with a smile. He went into the room and grabbed his gun.

"You going home?" his mom asked when he came out the room.

"Yeah, I gotta make sure Carl's there and grab something to eat."

"I made pork chops, gravy, and rice if you want some," she told him.

"Another time, Momma," he said and saw the disappointment on her face.

"Cook for me tomorrow. I'll bring Carl by and we'll have dinner together," he said, and she smiled.

"All right. You be careful."

"See you later, Momma. Bye Daddy," Carmelo said as he walked out the door.

# Chapter 56

---

# Brian

Carmelo walked into the apartment in Northeast and found B-Dog sleep on the couch. He sat in the loveseat opposite of him and waited for him to wake up.

"I thought you'd be in therapy by now," Brian yawned and stretched.

"Nah, I did that two nights ago with my mom," Carmelo told him. "How is she?"

"Who?"

"I don't know," Carmelo said, not knowing who he was more concerned about. "One of them. Both of them. Tell me something." He was frustrated, but B-Dog didn't answer. "How's my daughter?"

"She's fine. She asked about you yesterday."

"And?"

"I told her you'd call her soon."

"What about now?" Carmelo asked.

"All right," Brian said and reached for the phone.

"How's Maria?"

"I don't know."

"What you mean, you don't know? How could you not know?"

"Because Melinda kicked me out and I've been here for the past two days."

"So, we're both in the doghouse, huh?" Carmelo shook his head.

"Mine is only temporary," Brian told him.

Carmelo shook his head and took a deep breath.

"So, how's your granny?" Carmelo asked, changing the subject.

"She woke up yesterday."

"That's good news."

"What happened with your daughter?"

"She's all good," Carmelo told him. "Her birthday is on the fourth, but since it's on a Wednesday, we're having her birthday Saturday. I want Carmella to come, and I want to keep her for the weekend. Spend some time with her."

"I'll see what I can do," Brian said after a moment.

"See what you can do?" Carmelo was angry. "Dog, your cousin is bogus. You know it, and I know it. All I want to do is get to know my daughter and for my family to get to know her. My mom runs a daycare, and all my kids go there. I want her to know my family."

Brian was quiet for a minute.

"You're right my nigga. I'll make it happen," he said, and they watched TV in silence.

# Chapter 57

# Carmella

Carmelo cleaned Bunny's apartment and stocked the fridge. He wanted to call Brandy and ask what Carmella liked, but he didn't want to see her, let alone talk to her.

He was meeting Brian at Tanya's at 11:30.

"Hey," he greeted Tanya and Brian when he walked in.

"What's up, nigga?" Brian asked.

"Hey, Carmelo."

He looked down to see his daughter staring at him. They smiled at each other.

"You ready?" he asked, and she nodded.

Carmella walked to him and grabbed his hand.

"Is that her bag?"

"Yeah," Tanya handed it to him.

"I'll bring her back Sunday," he told them as they walked out the door.

The whole weekend Carmella would not leave his side. Two peas in a pod, they were. He took her shopping, and they ate in the food court. She was shy and didn't say much. She didn't let go of his hand either. He took her to meet her family. Her grandparents, her siblings, her uncles, and aunts.

At Ciara's birthday party, Carmella loosened up as long as she could see him. He took her to church on Sunday and didn't want to call B-Dog, but it wasn't his fault, and they had to make the best of the situation.

"You ready to bring her home?" he asked.

"No," Carmelo answered honestly. "But I am."

"I'm doing something right now. Tanya's at home."

"Hey, Carmelo. Come in." Tanya opened the door and moved out the way to let them in. "Hey, Carmella."

"Hi, Tanya," Carmella responded.

"Have a seat," Tanya told them.

Carmelo and Carmella sat on the sofa across from Tanya. She wore red leggings with a red, white, and blue shirt. She lifted her shirt up a little before she sat down and left her legs open, showing Carmelo her camel toe.

He looked up and saw her staring at him with a wicked grin on her face. *She knew what she was doing.* Although Carmelo hadn't had anyone as bad as Tanya besides Maria, he wasn't going to fall for it. He wanted her to fiend for him, so he sat back.

"Did you have fun?" she asked them.

"Yeah," Carmelo told her, and Carmella smiled.

"You don't have to be shy with me, Carmella. You're never shy with me," she told her, and Carmella leaned her body toward her dad.

"She loves you," Tanya told Carmelo. "You can tell."

"I love her. More than she knows," he said, putting his arms around her.

Tanya became envious, she wished her baby's father would have the same feelings for Jamie that Carmelo had for Carmella.

She began looking at Carmelo in a different light. She respected him now. She might even like him a little bit; she didn't know yet. Regardless, she was still going to fuck him. Carmelo's pager went off. He looked at it and stood. He knelt in front of his daughter.

"Daddy's gotta go. I'll call you tonight, and I'll see you at Granny's tomorrow. Okay?"

"Okay, Daddy," she told him. He opened his arms and they hugged.

"I love you, Angel," he told her.

"I love you, too."

"Let me walk you to the door," Tanya said as she got up.

"Nah, I'm good." Carmelo walked to the door and left.

Tanya sat on the couch and watched Carmella stare out the window as her dad pulled away. *He's playing hard to get*, she thought to herself. *We'll see how long that lasts.*

# Chapter 58

# Carmelo

In June, Carmelo and Carmella dropped Carl off in Bloomington and drove to Kankakee so she could meet her great grandma.

Carmelo's pager started blowing up the second day he was there. He called Bunny back first.

"What's up?"

"The police just locked up eight of the homies for murders," she said.

Carmelo wondered why she was calling him with this information. He wasn't a Blood.

"You're good, right? You and J.R." he asked her.

"Yeah, we're fine."

"All right, you straight? You need anything?"

"Yeah, I need you to stay in Illinois."

"Why?"

"Because the police are looking for you."

"What? Who told you that?"

"A lot of the homies did. They raided Wiz's pad and had like five or six of the homies on the ground and they were seeing if you were one of them."

"Damn. I'll call you back." Carmelo ended the call. "Grandma, we have to go."

"Is everything okay?"

"Yeah, Grandma. Everything is okay. I'll bring her back down here soon to see you."

"She's a sweetheart, Carmelo. You have a beautiful daughter."

"Thank you, Grandma. Carmella, go give grandma a hug."

Carmelo got on the highway after they left his grandma's. He pulled in front of Tanya's house at two in the morning. Carmella was asleep and he carried her into the house and followed Tanya to the spare bedroom. She wore a black transparent lingerie bra and panty set under an open robe. Carmelo could see the light bush through her panties and her light brown nipples. He laid his daughter down, walked out the room, and closed the door.

"Carmelo," Tanya called out his name when she saw him walking towards the door. "You just drove eight hours; you can stay the night."

Carmelo turned and saw Tanya standing with her hands on her hips, and robe wide open.

"Nah, I'm on one. I gotta go."

"You're scared of me, aren't you?"

Carmelo smiled to himself. The one thing he was great at was pussy. He could fuck good, and he could make a woman cum with his fingers. Tanya walked to him and put her hands around his neck.

"That's better," she said.

He reached up and grabbed her hands, took them from around his neck, and put them at her side.

"Keep them there," he said, seductively.

Carmelo rubbed his right hand down the side of her face, to her neck. He softly went down to the center of her breast, around her left nipple, and down her stomach. He went over her panty line.

"Spread your legs," he whispered, not looking at her.

When she did, he slid his middle and ring fingers inside of her. She was wet. She pushed her pelvis forward and he began rubbing his thumb on her clitoris in a circular motion. Tanya put her hands on his shoulders and arched her pelvis towards him. He knew what he was doing and was going to prove it.

"Carmelo, don't stop," she whispered but he ignored her.

He moved his fingers back and forth inside of her.

"Don't stop," she was breathing fast. "Don't stop."

Carmelo got her on the brink of an orgasm and stopped. He took his hands from between her legs and licked them. Tanya stared at him with her eyes full of lust. Carmelo turned and left, not once looking back.

# Chapter 59

---

# Carmelo

Carmelo grabbed the two black bags from the apartment in Northeast and drove to the spot on 31st and 12th. Cliff was sitting on the couch playing a video game when Carmelo walked in. He set the bags on the table and sat across from Cliff.

"The police are looking for me, so I might be going up for a while."

"I heard, A."

"Whatever happens, make sure that my kids are good. I'll be straight, I got these women and know how to survive in any environment." Carmelo told him. "I taught you what you needed to know, so there are no excuses. I got lucky, a nigga gave me two kilos of dope and six guns a year and a half ago and I ain't look back. I ain't never fell off, and I put niggas in good positions.

"We grew together, and we're making money. I'm giving you five kilos and eight heats. Show me what you can do with it. I'm leaving you in charge of this. Act like a leader and don't forget what I taught you. Don't forget where you came from or how far you've gotten. It wasn't fun being broke, so enjoy your life. The apartment is paid for until the end of the year; however, come January, I want everything moved out of both pads. I gave you all you need. Take care of each other."

Carmelo stood and left.

He drove to Nena's house to see his daughter and give her some money.

# Chapter 60

## Detective Turner

Detectives Turner and Young were staked outside Short Dog aunt's house on 29th and Park Avenue looking for any sign of him. He was wanted for two murders and known to visit this house frequently.

It was sad how one man could bring down a whole empire. Max B was caught for armed robbery. He was already a felon and looking at doing a substantial amount of time. He was offered twelve years and with good behavior out in eight, but that was too much time for the gang member. Instead, he decided to snitch for sixty months. Out of the ten men he snitched on, eight were in custody and two men were still at large.

Detective Turner had to piss. He walked into Clark's Gas Station and asked for the key. As he turned to walk out the door he froze. Carmelo Graham was driving down Park Avenue. His bladder could wait. He ran outside in time to see him park in front of Short Dog aunt's house. *Today was his lucky day*, he thought, as he jogged back to his car.

"Hey, baby," Carmelo kissed Nena as he walked into the house.
"Hey."

She was eight months pregnant, and it went good with her little frame.

"How's the baby doing?" he asked and touched her stomach.

"She's ready to come out, and I'm ready for her to come out," she said, and he laughed.

Carmelo's daughter kicked her mom's stomach and his eyes lit up.

"I told you," Nena said.

"Clarity's going to be a fighter."

"Clarity's going to be getting a lot of whippings," she said and chuckled.

"You better leave my baby alone," he told her with a smile.

"She better leave me alone and act right," Nena told him and smiled back.

Carmelo sat on the couch and relaxed. He handed Nena a ziplock bag of money.

"What's this for?"

"For you and Clarity."

"I have like twelve thousand put up that you gave me already."

"Add that to it, that's another ten. Hopefully, I beat this shit and won't be gone long."

"Beat what?" she asked and heard the knock on the door.

Carmelo knew that knock and closed his eyes.

"Carmelo, what's going on?" Nena demanded.

"That's the police outside. They probably saw me pull up."

"What do I do?"

"Come to the door with me. If they see we're together, they won't try no stupid shit."

He knew the house was surrounded so trying to run was pointless, plus, he was innocent.

When Nena opened the door, Carmelo saw Detectives Turner and Young with three more Officers and a K9. He was smart not to run.

"Carmelo Graham, you're under arrest," Detective Young said. "Step out and put your hands behind your back."

# Chapter 61

---

# Carmelo

Carmelo knew the routine. The handcuffs were put on tight, he was put inside of a squad car, and transported to the Hennepin County Jail.

Carmelo was placed in a holding cell by himself. The cell was filthy. It had apple cores, milk cartons, and pieces of bologna on the floor and a slab where a person sits. It smelled of strong urine and feet. Carmelo stood by the door and looked out the small window. His mind was somewhere else. They say in the end you think about the beginning, and for him, this was his end.

Carmelo didn't regret the past year and a half. That's not what got him there. It was the shit he did before he hooked up with B-Dog that landed him there. He didn't even regret that, because J.J. was his best friend, and Carmelo hoped that if somebody smoked him, one of his niggas would do the same.

He wondered if he did enough. If what he left was enough. His kids were young, and he wished he would have held them more and spent more time with them. *Did I love them enough? Would they remember me in five years? I just got to know Carmella; would she understand? I have three kids yet to be born. Will I ever get to hold them? Will they know that I loved them before they were born? Would they know me? That I was their father, or would they call somebody else 'Dad?'*

*I know Nena will take my daughter to my mom's, but what about Maria? Would she? Maria... Maria... Will she forgive me? Will I ever get the chance to apologize to her? Hug her again?* His thoughts flowed.

Carmelo was photographed, told his charges, and given a court date. He called his mom with his one free phone call.

"Hey, baby, how are you doing?" she asked him.

"I'm good," he told her. "Where's Daddy?"

"Right here, you want to talk to him?"

"Yeah," he said, and she put him on the phone.

"Hey, boy, what's up?"

"I'm locked up," Carmelo told his dad.

"For what?"

"Murder."

"When?"

"I don't know," Carmelo said. "I go to court tomorrow morning. I need you to get me a lawyer. Crystal, Jenny, and Bunny have the money."

"You downtown?"

"Yeah."

"What time is court tomorrow?"

"I don't want you to come. Just get me a lawyer," Carmelo told his dad, and he was quiet for a while.

"I'll get on that first thing in the morning."

"Alright, I gotta go," Carmelo said and was about to hang up.

"Hey, boy," his dad said. "You take care of yourself."

"I will."

Carmelo changed into green scrubs, and two hours later, he was escorted upstairs. He had only been to the juvenile detention center. Being in the County with a bunch of grown muthafuckas was new to him.

The unit they put him in had one Native and one White man in it, the rest were all niggas. They were playing Spades, Dominoes, talking on the phone, working out on the floor, watching TV, or in cells talking. Most of the cells were double bunked, and he was happy that his cell wasn't. It was overcrowded and there were blue beds on the dayroom floor. There were about forty men in a pod made for twenty-five.

Carmelo went into his room and closed the door. He made his bed and laid in it. It was already nine o'clock at night, and he'd been in booking for almost eight hours.

Carmelo stared at the ceiling in disbelief. At ten o'clock, an older brother knocked on his door and told him it was count time. Carmelo stepped outside the door and saw everybody lined up and followed suit. As the guard walked around with his clipboard getting everyone's name, Carmelo looked around for a familiar face. He saw a few people he knew, but no one of importance. When the count was done, the doors were closed, and the lights were turned out.

"Yo, shorty," Carmelo heard somebody say and looked up.

"What's up?"

"You want your food slot opened?" he asked.

"Yeah," Carmelo told him. The air felt good. It had been a long day. Carmelo closed his eyes and slept like a rock.

# Chapter 62

## Maria

*F*uck, Maria thought, *who keeps calling my fucking house this early in the morning?* She got out of bed and answered the phone. She had to pee anyway.

"Hello?"

"Wake up," Melinda told her.

"What? Is everything alright?" Maria asked, now wide awake.

"I wanted to tell you before you saw it on the news," Melinda said, and Maria's heart skipped a beat.

"What?" she panicked.

"Carmelo's locked up," Melinda said.

Maria was speechless. She hadn't talked to him since the day at the hospital. She thought about him like crazy. She still loved him but was mad that he lied. He told her that he sold drugs, so why lie about a name or having kids.

"What did he do?" she found herself asking her sister.

"He killed somebody," Melinda said.

Maria was quiet for a while. She was going to have his baby in two months. Chloe was the name he wanted. They made so many plans.

"Hello?"

"I'm here," Maria assured her sister.

"How are you doing?"

"I'm in shock," Maria said and sat in thought for a minute. "I still love him, Mel."

"I know."

"How's Brian doing?"

"He's up."

"This early?" Maria asked, surprised.

"Yeah, I told him when I saw it on the news."

"What'd he say?" Maria asked, curiously.

"Nothing. He got up and grabbed the phone book."

"Grabbed the phone book? Why!"

"To get Carmelo a lawyer," Melinda said and neither one of them spoke.

"He really loves him, huh?"

"Yeah, he does. I like him too. I just don't like what he did to you."

"I know."

"Well, I'm going to let you go, Maria. I just thought you should know," Melinda said.

"Thanks, Mel."

"Anytime." Melinda was about to hang up.

"Mel!" Maria yelled.

"Yeah, sweety."

"Tell Brian if he needs any help paying to call me."

"I will," Melinda said and hung up.

# Chapter 63

---

# Carmelo

The next morning, the lights were turned on at 5:30 a.m. Carmelo heard his door buzz open. He opened his eyes and stared at the ceiling. It wasn't a dream. He was really in the county jail.

Carmelo heard a knock on the door and looked up.

"They're about to serve breakfast," an older Black man told him.

Carmelo got up, expecting cereal, eggs, and toast like he got when he was in juvenile. He saw people standing in a line by the door and followed suit. Ten minutes later a guard entered the sallyport with a cart. He was given two Elfin loaves, an orange, and a milk. Carmelo got his and went back to his cell to eat. Twenty minutes later, he heard his name being called over the loudspeaker.

"Graham, get ready for court. You have five minutes."

Carmelo brushed his teeth, then sat back on the bed. He was getting lost in his own thoughts when he heard a lot of noise outside the door. It sounded like metal chains hitting each other.

"Graham to the door," he heard over the speaker. Carmelo got up and walked to the main door.

"You're about to be a part of the chain gang, shorty," he heard somebody say, then the door was buzzed.

Carmelo walked into the hallway where there were about twenty people in a line, cuffed two by two. Carmelo looked down the line for a familiar face and caught Short Dog's eye.

"What's up, my nigga?" Carmelo asked.

"Shit Blood, they caught me going to my baby mom's pad."

"They caught me at your aunt's house."

"Yeah, I know. I called over there and they told me. I tried to duck into my baby mom's pad last night. They were waiting."

"You got here last night?"

"Yeah, they caught me a little after nine and held me at the homicide office for a half an hour until I told them I wanted a lawyer."

"Name," the guard interrupted them.

"Graham."

"Hogan."

In the hallway, they were cuffed together and placed in the back of the line.

"That's everybody," the deputy said, and they began walking down the hallway.

After walking for what seemed like a mile underground, the deputy stopped at a locked door. There were three bullpens. The first was for female offenders, the second was for drug court, and the third was for male offenders. The bullpen was already half full and Carmelo looked in to see if he recognized anybody. He saw some Bogus Boys, Family Mob, and Crips standing by each other and prepared mentally for a fight. He wasn't too worried, because, besides Short Dog, there were two more Bloods in the bullpen.

"What's up, Blood?" Short Dog greeted the two men when they walked in.

"Menace, what's up, lil' nigga? What you doing down here, lil' Blood?" one of them asked.

Carmelo was used to them calling him Blood, they'd been doing it since he was a kid. The four of them walked to a corner so they could talk.

"They got me for a murder," Carmelo told them.

"Max B bitch ass telling on you too?"

"I don't know. I just got down here. I ain't seen no paperwork yet."

"You make sure when you see that public pretender of a lawyer, you ask him to put in a motion for your Discovery. That'll tell you everybody on your case and if anybody said anything."

"I'm getting a lawyer, but I'm going to make sure I do that."

The door opened and a few more people came in. Carmelo looked and saw two niggas from Bogus he got into it with on the streets talking to some Crips and looking at him. He stood to the side so he could watch them.

"What's up?" Short Dog asked.

"The Bootsie niggas keep looking over here," Carmelo told him.

"What's up, Menace? You got beef with one of them?"

"Fuck them niggaz," Carmelo said. "I'm down here right now for one of them."

"You good, lil' Blood?" Short Dog asked. "We could beat their ass right now."

"Nah, I'm good."

At nine o'clock, the deputies began calling names and sending people upstairs to court. First Monte, then Short Dog, then Bugz. Carmelo went last.

When Carmelo walked into the courtroom the seats were filled. He stood at the podium in front of the judge, not knowing what to expect.

"Dan Goetz for the State."

"Alex Perez for the defendant."

Carmelo wasn't listening to the prosecutor. He was looking at his lawyer. He was facing life in prison and it didn't matter.

Alex Perez stood five foot four with big brown eyes, full lips, and long hair in a ponytail. She wore a gray two-piece dress suit with a white blouse, unbuttoned at the top. Her coat was tight around her middle and her breast was perfect. Her skirt stopped at her knees. Her ass was round, her calves were well defined, and she wore a pair of white and gray heels.

"Hello, Mr. Graham," the judge said.

"Hello, Your Honor," Carmelo responded.

"Do you understand why you're here?"

"Yes."

"Your lawyer and the prosecutor are going to argue your bail. If you have any questions, raise your hand, and I'll give you some time to confer with your lawyer."

"Okay."

Carmelo listened to his lawyer and prosecutor go back and forth, arguing over what his bail should be. He knew the judge wasn't going to let him go, he was down for a murder.

The judge made his bail five hundred thousand dollars, and a court date was set.

"I'll be back to see you tomorrow. Don't talk to anyone about your case," Alex told him before he was escorted out the courtroom.

When Carmelo walked into the bullpen, it was almost empty. The deputy handed him an apple, milk, and two bologna sandwiches for lunch. He had just finished eating when he saw the two niggas from Bogus stepping out of the elevator. When they saw him, they looked at each other and smiled. Carmelo knew what time it was and walked toward the door. When the deputy uncuffed the first one, Carmelo rushed him. He scooped him and slammed him hard on the ground and began punching him in the face. The deputy got on her walkie-talkie to call for backup, letting go of the other one, who rushed in and hit Carmelo on the side of the head. Carmelo rolled and got to his feet fast. He knew if he stayed down, it was over.

The mace hit him as he got to his feet, and he heard the deputies running. Carmelo couldn't see and fell into the fetal position. A deputy got on top of him and cuffed him.

# Chapter 64

---

# Alex Perez

Carmelo woke in the empty cell and looked around the room. *So this is what I got to look forward to*, he thought. He stared at the wall, the toilet connected to the sink, and then the floor. He had two apartments out there, but it all meant nothing here.

His thoughts were interrupted. He had a visit. Two deputies escorted him to the lawyer/client visiting room where Alex Perez sat next to an older White man.

"Hi, my name is Richard Williams. I'm with the firm, Williams, Smith, and Schmidt. Your dad hired me," the older man said, extending his hand.

"What's up?" Carmelo replied, shaking the older man's hand.

"Hi Carmelo," Alex greeted him with a smile.

"Hi. How are you?"

"Fine, thank you," she said. "There seems to be a problem. Your brother Brian hired me to represent you, and your parents hired Mr. Williams and his firm. You have to choose which one of us you'd like to represent you."

Carmelo didn't know B-Dog hired Alex. He asked his dad to get him a lawyer because he didn't expect anyone else to do it. He trusted B-Dog's judgment because he lived the street life and chose to go with Alex.

"Thank you for coming," Carmelo said to Richard. "But I'm going to stick with her."

"No problem. I'll give your parents back their money. You have a nice day," Richard said and knocked on the door.

"Now that that is settled," Alex said when Richard left, "I looked at your case, and they really don't have too much to go on besides Maxwell Baker. They have no gun, no evidence, nothing but hearsay. They also have a guy named Chris Light, a.k.a. Mr. Mad Rollin, who placed you at the scene, but he's a gang member and by himself isn't enough. Now you add Maxwell Baker, who also has a motive to lie, and they have a case."

Carmelo listened as his attorney explained what she knew.

"The homicide detectives say there are rumors on the street, but no one is willing to come forward officially. It's all circumstantial and hearsay besides Mr. Light. We have an evidentiary hearing next month, and I'm going to try to get Maxwell's statement thrown out. If I can do that, then you'll be released. If not, we go to trial. Any questions?"

"Can we win?" Carmelo asked, locking eyes with the lawyer.

"Yes," she told him, returning his stare.

She gave him her business card. They shook hands and she left.

Carmelo stared at the card while he waited for the deputy to come back for him. *Alex Perez. Ms. Alex Perez. Single Alex Perez. Sexy Alex Perez. Beautiful Alex Perez.*

# Chapter 65

## Cliff

When Cliff heard Carmelo was locked up, he sat DeWayne and Jamal down.

"Yo, my niggas, it's just us now. Menace is gone and might be for a long time. He taught us everything we need to know. We've held down spots, and now, we have to grow up. All the bullshit we used to do has to stop. The rent is paid for the next six months, which means we have six months to blow up and branch out."

"Who are we supposed to buy our goods from?" DeWayne asked. "Menace used to supply us. Do we know who he got his goods from?"

"When we get to that point, we'll deal with it. Menace left us five bricks," Cliff told them.

"You for real?" Jamal asked.

"Yeah, nigga, I'm for real," Cliff said. "We're not going to trick this shit off either. I'm not ever going back to being broke. So, if you're on some bullshit let me know now, we'll split this shit up and I'll leave."

"We have to give Menace's mom twenty thousand out of every brick," Cliff said when nobody spoke. "We'll get twelve ounces a piece and give her seven thousand each. With the rest of our money, shit, let's put some of it to the side until we find a nigga willing to fuck with us."

"I got a cousin who sells good dope. He's a Blood nigga too, from the hood. We can holla at him," Jamal told them.

"Where's he at?" Cliff asked.

"He stays on 37th and 3rd Avenue, across the street from Sabathani."

"Let's go holler at him," Cliff said and grabbed his .40 caliber pistol.

They got on their bikes and headed to the hood.

They were at the stoplight on 35th and 4th when Chad pulled up on the side of them with the twins, Anthony and Antonio, in a stolen car.

"What's up, Cliff, DeWayne, Mal? What you niggas up to?" Chad asked and Cliff looked inside the car.

"Nigga, you still stealing cars?" Cliff shook his head. "We're on something, my nigga. When y'all grow up and get tired of being broke and want to get some of this dough, come holla at us."

Cliff, Dewayne, and Jamal rode off.

"We're not going to let this nigga know shit." Cliff told them when they were in front of the house. "I know this is your cousin, Jamal. But we're not telling him what we do or don't do. We're asking questions, that's all. Cool?"

"Cool," Jamal said and knocked on the door.

"Who is it?"

"Jamal."

"What's up, lil' nigga?"

"This is Cliff and DeWayne," Jamal said, making introductions. "This is my cousin, RedRum."

"Y'all smoke?" RedRum asked as he blazed up a blunt.

"Nah, we're good," Cliff answered for all of them.

"So, what's up?" RedRum asked.

"We're trying to buy some goods."

RedRum choked. "What?"

"We're trying to buy some goods," Cliff repeated.

"Y'all serious, huh?"

"Yeah, we are."

"What do y'all know about goods?"

"We know enough," Cliff said. "We've had our own spot, so we know what we're doing."

"How old are you?"

"Fifteen."

"And you've had your own spot?"

"Yeah."

"What do you know?"

"We know what we're doing," Cliff assured him.

"Why'd you come to me?" RedRum talked directly to Cliff.

"Because you're Jamal's relative, which means you wouldn't try to jack us or let somebody else try to, and we won't have to kill anybody." Cliff looked RedRum in the eye.

"So, what are y'all trying to cop? An eight ball, quad, ounce?" he asked, ignoring Cliff's comment.

"A bird," Cliff said and RedRum choked for the second time.

"Lil niggas, get the fuck out of my house. Playing games with me and shit!" he yelled, and no one moved. "Do you know how much a kilo cost?"

"No."

"Twenty thousand. That's dollars nigga. Twenty thousand dollars."

"So, if we bring you twenty thousand dollars," Cliff said, pausing like RedRum did. "You'll sell us a bird?"

"Bring me the twenty," he told Cliff and put the blunt in his mouth.

# Chapter 66

---

# Cliff

Two days later, the twins paged Cliff.

"Hello?"

"It's Antonio."

"What's up, my nigga?"

"Shit. Just calling to say what's up."

"Oh okay. I'm on my way to this bitch's pad."

"You told us to call you if we wanted to make money."

Cliff smiled to himself. *The pussy would have to wait.*

"Yeah, I did," he said. "Where y'all at?"

"We're at my pad."

"Who's all over there?"

"Just me, my brother, and Chad."

"Where's your mom and little brother?"

"Gone."

"We're on our way," Cliff said and hung up.

"We have to stop by the Twin's pad," he told DeWayne and Jamal.

"Why?" Jamal asked. He wanted some pussy.

"They took us up on our offer."

"Was Chad with them?" DeWayne asked.

"Yep, they're together."

"Can we trust them?" Jamal asked.

"Especially Chad, stealing and doing dumb shit," DeWayne said.

"We'll soon find out," Cliff told them as they headed for the Twin's pad.

Antonio and Chad were playing Sega Genesis and Anthony was on the couch watching when they walked into the house.

"Turn the game off," DeWayne told Antonio.

"Tonio said y'all wanted to get down," Cliff looked at them one at a time.

"Yeah, we do," Anthony spoke up.

"What about you, Chad?" Cliff asked.

"Yeah, me too."

"Alright, my nigga. The only reason why I'm going along with this is because the way we grew up was fucked up," Cliff told them. "We ain't never have shit, whether it was food or clothes. Plus, none of y'all niggas ever became Bloods. The nigga who put us on said that we weren't a gang, and we're not turning it into one. Our only focus is getting this bread. I know none of y'all niggas ever sold dope, 'cause we've been around each other too long. Now, there's three of us and three of y'all. Chad, you're going to come with me, Antonio, DeWayne's going to fuck with you, and Jamal, you got Anthony."

"Cool," Jamal said.

"No more stealing cars," Cliff said, and Chad gave him a mischievous look. "Nigga, I'm serious. The shit we're doing don't need attention, and if you're going to fuck with us, I'm not going to let you do shit that's going to put us at risk."

They all stared at Chad.

"Okay."

"Now, I'm going to give y'all three ounces a piece. Off that, you'll make around seventy-five hundred. You'll give me twenty-five of that." He looked at them and saw they were listening and continued. "If you fuck up, I get twenty-five hundred. If you lose your goods, I get twenty-five hundred. If you trick off, I get twenty-five hundred. Understand so far?"

"Why are we giving you twenty-five hundred?" Chad asked.

"Because I'm not giving you this shit for free, nigga. We gotta buy it, so you gotta buy it. We're in this together now. We look out for each other, and we take care of each other. There's only one rule, you snitch, you die.

"There's no excuses. We all know where each other live; we all know each other's family. That goes for all of us, me too. So, know what you're doing before you start because I will not hesitate to kill any one of y'all if y'all snitch. Understood?"

Chad, Antonio, and Anthony nodded.

# Chapter 67

## Chris

Chris and Mark were buying a quarter of a kilo a month and living the good life. They were watching television when Chris's pager vibrated. It was his oldest brother C.J.

"What's up, nigga?" Chris asked.

"Shit. Where you at?"

"I'm at the spot. What's up?"

"I need you to run me to Eau Claire, Wisconsin."

Chris started laughing. "Nigga, you want me to drive you to Wisconsin?"

"Yeah, nigga. I'll pay you, lil' nigga, but I gotta leave tonight."

"Shorty," Chris turned to Mark.

"What's up, Maniac?"

"You want to go to Wisconsin for the night?"

"I don't give a fuck."

"Give us an hour," Chris told C.J. and hung up.

◆ ◆ ◆ ◆

There was a party going on at the address C.J. gave him.

"Is this where you're staying?" Chris asked.

"Yeah. My White bitch lives here."

"Shit, we're coming in."

"I don't care. Come on."

Chris and Mark followed C.J. into the house.

C.J. disappeared, leaving Chris and Mark to fend for themselves.

"Hey, bro," a white dude said as he tapped Chris on the shoulder.

"What's up?" Chris asked.

"You got some blow?"

"Some what?"

"Some blow. Some coke?" the white guy yelled into his ear.

"Yeah, I do."

"Cool. How much?"

"A hundred dollars a gram."

"Let me get one."

"Alright. Let's go outside."

Chris had an ounce of cocaine in his car. He took out a scale and weighed a gram. He ripped a piece of a baggie to put it in and handed it to the white dude.

"What's your name, bro?" the white guy asked as he handed Chris the hundred-dollar bill.

"Maniac."

"I'm John."

John came back to see Chris three more times, each time bringing two or three of his buddies. Chris sold the ounce in two hours.

"We're moving to Eau Claire." Chris told Mark on the drive back to Minneapolis. "It's too much money out here cousin. I just sold an ounce in less than two hours."

"I was going to tell you the same thing. I was in the bathroom getting my dick sucked by this thick corn-fed white bitch."

"Fuck the bitches cousin. Did you know that the pills we sell for twenty dollars in Minneapolis goes for fifty up here?" Chris was excited. "Do you know how much money we can make down here?"

Chris was tired of dealing with the fiends in Minneapolis. If it wasn't three for fifty, it was six for a hundred, or fifteen for a pill. Somebody was always trying to get over.

Chris didn't hear one complaint from the white boys, and nobody came up short.

# Chapter 68

# Carmelo

Carmelo spent twenty-one days in segregation, then moved to quad 4B and double-bunked with P-Funk, a Piru from California.

"What's up, Blood?" P-Funk got off the bed to greet him.

"What's up, Funk?"

"Damn, I'm happy they put you in here instead of a weirdo, Blood. You need anything?"

"Nah, I got money. I'm good."

"Blood, whatever is in here, you can have. I don't even eat half this shit. This is my winnings from gambling these niggas. They're sweet as hell, Blood. On Piiiiru."

"Good looking, bro." Carmelo made his bed and prepared for the long haul.

He went to court a month later and a trial date was set. Carmelo sat in the bullpen frustrated. His motion was denied, and trial wasn't for another sixty days. Bunny had given birth to his daughter, Carmen, and he had another daughter, Clarity, born by

Nena. The thought of not being able to watch his kids grow up was the foundation of his frustration.

Carmelo wasn't with his kids every night to read bedtime stories or tuck them in. He didn't eat breakfast with them or drop them off to school or daycare either, but he didn't look at himself as being a deadbeat dad. Carmelo provided for his kids. He paid rent and mortgages, he bought food and clothes, and he spent as much time as he could with them. The good thing about the unit was a lot of the niggas in there didn't use the phone in the daytime, allowing Carmelo to spend hours talking with the people he loved.

"Yo, Menace!" P-Funk called out.

"What's up?"

Carmelo hung the phone up and walked to the table.

"Yo, Blood, you know how to play spades?"

"Yeah. I've been playing spades my whole life."

"I need you to be my spade's partner."

"Cool."

"This is Rick G and Tim," P-Funk said, introducing them. "This is my homeboy, Menace."

Carmelo and P-Funk won the first three games and were down 23 to 12 in the fourth.

"Give us ten," P-Funk said as he began to deal.

Carmelo looked at his first four cards. Four spades, the King, Queen, and two smaller ones, and waited until the deal was done to look at the rest. The game went to twenty-six and their opponents needed four. P-Funk picked up his hand, looked at it, and smiled.

"Your play," he said to Rick G, who ignored him.

"How many you got Tim?" Rick G asked his partner.

"None."

Rick G looked at P-Funk. "You set the deck, nigga."

"I ain't set shit, nigga," P-Funk told him. "Don't get mad because you're set, nigga. Lose like a man and go get my shit."

"You cheated, nigga, and I ain't paying you shit," Rick G said and stood up.

P-Funk hit Rick in the stomach, and he curled up. Carmelo hit him in the face, and they began punching Rick G until he fell. They wore flip flops and stomped on his face and body instead of kicking him.

"You got a problem too, nigga?" P-Funk asked Tim.

"Hell nah, bruh. That ain't my business."

P-Funk walked into Rick G's cell and took his commissary.

"Nigga, you better not say shit," he told Rick G as he walked past him.

Rick G wrote a kite and was gone the next morning.

# Chapter 69

# Cliff & DeWayne

"We smoke, we fuck, and we're out of here," Cliff told DeWayne as they were putting their bikes on the porch.

"Cool."

"Hey, Cliff. DeWayne," the girl said when she opened the door.

"What's up, Ann?" Cliff said and hugged her.

"Where's Keisha?" Dewayne asked as they walked into the house.

"She's coming. She's upstairs."

"Oh, okay."

They walked into the living room and sat on the couch. Cliff pulled a bag of weed out and began rolling a blunt. Ann turned the TV on the Jukebox channel and turned the volume up.

"What's up, Keisha?" DeWayne asked when she walked down the stairs.

"Hey, DeWayne," Keisha hugged him. "What's up, Cliff?"

"What's up, Key?"

Cliff lit the blunt, took a few puffs, and passed it. They all smoked while the music played. When the blunt was gone, as if on cue, DeWayne stood and grabbed Keisha, leading her upstairs, leaving Cliff and Ann. *In and out*, he thought, as he climbed the stairs.

DeWayne got a page an hour later.

"I gotta go," he said to Keisha and began putting his clothes on.

"Damn, nigga, so you ain't got no time to chill with me?"

"Are you gon' pay me to chill with you?"

"What? Nigga, you got me fucked up. What you mean, pay you to chill?"

"Keisha," DeWayne said as he tied his shoe, "I know it wasn't my good looks that attracted you to me. It was the clothes I had on and the fact that I got money. We both know that. So, all this attitude you're portraying, miss me with that bullshit. Now, I gotta go make this money. Call me later if you want to."

DeWayne walked down the stairs and saw Cliff already dressed and ready to go.

In and out.

"Alright, Ann," DeWayne said and walked out the house.

Cliff and DeWayne were riding their bikes down 28th Street when DeWayne's pager went off.

Cliff saw a blue Regal drive past and looked at the occupants in the car. He knew he'd seen them before, but his mind was cloudy. That hoe Ann sat on him and rode him like a stallion, then, before he came, got off and put his dick in her mouth, swallowing his cum.

They were at the top of the bridge on 2nd Avenue when it came to him. *Ah fuck, the niggas were at Menace's court hearing.* He was already reaching for his heat when he heard the car.

DeWayne was on the sidewalk looking at his pager, oblivious of what was going on. It was like déjà vu. *First Menace, now DeWayne, these two niggas and these punk ass pagers.*

He leaned towards DeWayne, knocking him over when he felt the pain in his left arm. A bullet grazed his forehead, then he rapidly fired his gun. He saw the bullets hitting the car and then the door. He lifted his gun higher and seen the nigga leaning out the window duck back into the car, as they sped off. DeWayne pushed Cliff off of him.

"Nigga, you alright?" Cliff heard DeWayne ask, looking at him.

"Yeah, I'm good," he said. "The nigga shot me in the arm."

DeWayne grabbed Cliff's gun and put it on his waist. "Abbott's up the street, come on." DeWayne helped Cliff get on the handlebars and they rode to Abbott Northwestern Hospital.

DeWayne couldn't wait with Cliff at the ER. He carried two guns on him and dope. He made sure Cliff was alright and left.

DeWayne rode home with blood on his clothes. He was changing when Jamal walked in.

"What's up, nigga?"

"Them niggas shot Cliff," DeWayne told Jamal.

"What you say, nigga?" Jamal asked.

DeWayne had tears in his eyes. He and Cliff had been friends since the fourth grade. They'd both had rough childhoods. He knew Jamal, Chad, and the twins, but Cliff was his first friend and he loved him like a brother.

When Menace put them on and took them out of the fucked up life they were living, asking for nothing in return but loyalty, he promised to be loyal to him for life. He would have done anything Menace asked him to, no matter the price. Now today, Cliff put himself in front of a bullet for him, showing brotherly love. For these two niggas, he would go to hell for.

After DeWayne changed, he and Jamal rode to Abbott to check on Cliff. Detectives Turner and Young were talking to a nurse when they walked in. DeWayne and Jamal were about to turn around when Detective Young saw them and tapped Detective Turner.

"Well, well, well," Detective Young said and smiled, "if it isn't DeWayne. To what do we owe the pleasure? Are you here to see your friend?"

"He's alright. He has a bullet wound to the arm. He'll make it." Detective Turner chimed in. "How did you know that Cliff was here? He hasn't called anybody."

DeWayne and Jamal stood there without saying a word.

"We have one guy shot in the shoulder and upper chest. Another with glass in his eye from a shattered window who'll probably never see out of that eye. We have your guy with a bullet wound in his arm, a flesh wound across his forehead, and you, without a scratch.

"I wonder how that's possible. Were you hiding? Ducking under a car while your friend was getting shot? Were you peeing your pants, Mr. Simpson?" Detective Turner taunted.

"Where were you when this happened?" Detective Young asked.

"I want a lawyer."

"You're not under arrest," Detective Young said. "Or should you be?"

DeWayne didn't respond.

"Who's your friend?" Detective Turner asked. "What's your name?"

"Jamal Thomas."

"Where were you today?"

"I was with my lawyer."

"Another smart ass," Detective Turner said. "Well, smart ass one and two, Cliff is coming with us for the night."

He smiled and walked away.

# Chapter 70

## DeWayne & Cliff

That night, the five of them sat at the house.

"So, you didn't see who was dumping?" Chad asked.

"Nah, nigga. Cliff was on top of me," DeWayne told them again.

"So we don't know who the fuck was dumping at y'all or why?" Antonio asked.

"Nope."

"And they got Cliff downtown?" he asked again.

"Yep."

"So, we have to wait until we holla at him to know who we're beefing with?" Anthony asked.

"Yep," DeWayne said, and they all looked at him. He was their new leader.

"We're going to wait until we find out what's going on with Cliff. Whoever shot him is dead, that's my word. If y'all niggas ain't ready for war leave now, 'cause I swear to God once this war starts, if anyone of y'all snitch, I'm gonna personally smoke you.

"This nigga put his life on the line and took a bullet for me. He set the example and that's the example we follow. I'll protect you with my life, die for you, ride for you, and I expect the same. This shit don' got real. The money was the fun part, the killing is necessary. If y'all aren't ready, leave before it's too late," DeWayne told them and took a puff of the blunt.

◆ ◆ ◆ ◆

Cliff was released after thirty-six hours. When he walked into the apartment, DeWayne was sitting on the couch smoking a blunt and staring at the wall.

"What's up, my nigga?" Cliff said to him.

"What's up?" DeWayne smiled. "How you doing?"

"I'm okay. Where's everybody?"

"Jamal's at T.T.'s, the twins are at their pad, and Chad is somewhere booping probably." Cliff sat down. "We didn't know who did what and there wasn't no use for everybody to sit around, so I kicked 'em out and told 'em I'd call when I heard something."

"How you doing, bro?"

"I'm alright," DeWayne said, holding his emotions in. "Who we killing?"

"It was the niggas from Menace's court date."

You want me to call Mal?"

"Yeah."

Thirty minutes later, Jamal, Chad, and the twins were there.

"What's up, nigga?" Chad said as he walked through the door. "Who signed their death wish?"

Cliff was happy to see these niggas had his back. He didn't regret what he did. Now they looked up to him for direction. It was time to get respect from everybody else.

Cliff looked at Chad. "We're going to need some stolen cars."

# Chapter 71

---

# Brian

Brian sat at the pad in Northeast. It had been two days since Maria had her baby. Brian stood and watched her cry when the nurse asked where the father was.

He knew she missed Carmelo. She asked about him every time they saw one another. Brian hadn't talked to him since he'd been locked up and missed his lil' nigga too. He had two licks waiting for him and had to be patient.

Brian received Carmelo's Motion of Discovery and read it. Maxwell, he couldn't get, because he was locked up for the next two years. He read Mad Rollin's statement and memorized his address. He grabbed his gun and left.

Brian stalked Mad Rollin's house every night for two and a half weeks waiting for him to show up. Carmelo's trial was beginning soon. Brian crept further behind the bush as he saw headlights approaching. The car parked in front of the house, the music stopped, and the door opened.

Mad Rollin stepped out of the car and started walking toward the house when Brian came from behind the bushes and shot Mad Rollin twice in the back of the head.

# Chapter 72

# Assassins

The sling was off, and the war was on. They had inherited Menace's beef. Blood had been drawn and there was no backing down. Cliff created nicknames for them and a name for their crew. 187 Assassins. Cliff a.k.a. C.C., DeWayne a.k.a. Heartless, Jamal a.k.a. SouthSide, Chad a.k.a. Killa C, Anthony a.k.a. Cain, and Antonio a.k.a. Abel. Southside, C.C., and Heartless sat at Cousin Greg's while he went and tested the dope RedRum had given him.

"No good," Cousin Greg told them. "Y'all been jacked."

"You tried them both?" Southside asked.

"Yep, no good."

"Alright," C.C. said and grabbed the bag with the dope.

"Yo, A," he said to Southside when they were outside. "That's your cousin, A. Where you stand?"

"The nigga jacked me too, A. You know where I stand."

They drove to the spot in silence. Cain, Abel, and Killa C were waiting when they walked in.

"Grab y'all heat," C.C. told them.

"What's up? What happened, A.?" Killa C asked.

"The nigga RedRum jacked us for two kilos of dope," C.C. told them. Cain and Abel stood and went to grab their pistols.

"Yo, A., Killa C, Abel, Cain, y'all go to the back, we'll let you in. Wait for us and make sure nobody comes. Watch the front too," C.C told them when they pulled in front of RedRum's house.

C.C. waited until he was sure everybody was in position before he knocked on the door.

"What's up, lil' niggas? Y'all back already?"

"Where's our money?" C.C. asked.

"What you say, lil' nigga?"

"I said, where's our money," C.C. asked again.

"Y'all trippin'," RedRum said and attempted to shut the door.

Heartless pushed it open, causing RedRum to fall into the house. C.C. and Southside followed them in and closed the door.

"What the fuck?" RedRum said.

"Where. The. Fuck. Is. Our. Money?" C.C. emphasized.

"Nigga, I gave y'all the goods," RedRum said, and Southside threw the bag on the table.

"Cousin Greg said it was bullshit," Southside told him.

"That's what the nigga gave me."

"Well, somebody's gonna give us our money back, or we gon' have a dead muthafucka around here," C.C. said.

"Nigga, who the fuck . . ." RedRum began.

C.C., Heartless, and Southside pointed their pistols at him.

"Jamal. Relative," RedRum pleaded, "I gave y'all what the nigga gave me. I swear."

"Get him to come over, 'cause he gave you some bullshit."

RedRum reached for the phone and talked for a minute. "He'll be here in thirty minutes."

Forty minutes later there was a knock on the door. Southside went to answer it.

"Where's RedRum?" the man asked and walked into the house.

"What's up, my nigga?" he asked RedRum.

"What's up, Tone?"

"What you need?"

"We need our money or our two bricks of dope." C.C. stood.

"Who the fuck is this nigga?" he asked RedRum.

"I'm the nigga you sold the bogus shit to. RedRum bought the shit for us and it's bullshit, so either give us our muthafuckin' money or our two bricks."

Tone looked at C.C. "Nigga, I ain't giving you shit."

C.C. pulled his gun out and hit Tone across the face in one quick motion. He fell to the floor and saw blood come out his nose. When he looked up, there were three guns pointing at him.

"Shorty, I fucked up. I'm sorry," Tone pleaded. "Let me make things right. Give me twenty-four hours, and I'll give you three kilos of good coke."

"No. Give us our money now."

"I don't have it."

"So, you're willing to die over forty thousand dollars?" C.C. asked, pointing the gun at Tone.

"Hold on," he said. "I got it in my truck. It's in my truck."

"Let's go then."

C.C. followed Tone outside, while Southside and Heartless remained in the house.

Tone walked to the driver's side of his truck and opened it with C.C. directly behind him. He reached in and grabbed the bag on the back seat.

"Hand me the bag," C.C. said.

Tone turned around and looked at C.C. for a second, then handed him the bag.

"Come on, let's go back inside."

When they walked into the house, Killa C was standing over RedRum.

"What's up, A.? We good?"

"Yeah, we're good." C.C. said and then looked at Tone. "Hand me your keys."

"What?"

"Let me see your keys," he asked again.

When Tone handed C.C. the keys, he threw them to RedRum. "You have five minutes to move this truck away from your house."

RedRum looked at Tone one last time before walking out the door.

"Tone, we're keeping this. You're a bullshit ass nigga and you don't deserve it. I'm giving you your life though. Walk out that door and don't look back. You come back on bullshit; you won't leave again."

Tone was unsure and hesitant to move. He walked slowly toward the door backward.

Once outside, he turned and walked normal. *Who this nigga think he is, talking about don't come back,* Tone thought? *I'll be back all right. These lil' niggas are going to let me live? Jack me like I'm a bitch? Take my shit and slap me with the strap?* He walked up the street deep in thought. *I'm about to call my niggas and it's on.*

Tone walked to the corner of 38th and waited on the number #23 bus to come. It was taking too long, so he decided to walk towards Nicollet and hop on the number #18 bus.

He saw a young nigga coming out of the alley and tensed up. He took a deep breath when the lil' nigga walked past him. At the corner, he passed another lil' nigga and stopped. *Didn't I just pass this lil' nigga,* he thought and turned around. He saw both of them standing there . . . twins. Tone looked down and saw the pistols in their hands.

At that moment, Tone knew he hadn't gotten away and would never get revenge.

*Did I enjoy my life,* he thought in those few seconds? *Will somebody find the money I stashed in the house?* Crazy, the things people think about when they're facing death. He had a chance, slim as it may be. Tone turned around and began to run. He felt the first bullet hit him in the back, then the second. The third hit him in the neck, and then darkness overcame him.

# Chapter 73

---

# Carmelo

Monte was acquitted. Max B didn't hold up and Carmelo felt good. Short Dog had started trial and Carmelo's trial started in three weeks.

Alex came to see him later that day.

"Hi Carmelo," she greeted him when he entered the room.

"Hey, Alex. How are you doing?"

"I'm hopeful. A few things. Number one, Maxwell didn't do too well for the prosecution."

"I heard," Carmelo had a smile on his face.

"Have you seen the news?"

"No. Why?" Carmelo asked, skeptically.

"Chris Light was found murdered last night in front of his mom's house, and without him, they don't have a case. I've asked for another evidentiary-post trial hearing. We see the judge Tuesday."

"Six days from now?"

"Yes," she told him, and he smiled for the second time. "Don't get your hopes up, we still might have to go to trial."

Carmelo walked back to the quad on cloud nine. B-Dog did his job. Everything else was up to Alex.

◆ ◆ ◆ ◆

On Tuesday, Carmelo was up and ready for court. Short Dog was already in the hallway when he walked out, wearing a dark blue suit, white shirt, and red tie.

"You look sharp, nigga," Carmelo told him. "How's your trial going?"

"Real good. All they have is Max's bitch ass, and he ain't no good. My lawyer chopped him down crucially. They have two more people to testify against me, and then it's closing arguments. You know I ain't going to testify. My past is so fucked up, plus, it's all on them anyway."

"That's true, my nigga," Carmelo told him. "Good luck though, bro."

"Thanks, Blood. I appreciate it," Short Dog said. "Good luck to you, too."

Carmelo left for court a little while after Short Dog. He hadn't told anyone to come and wasn't expecting to see B-Dog there.

Alex wore a tan knee-length skirt and orange blouse with the top three buttons undone under a tan jacket. She leaned over to whisper something in his ear, and Carmelo could see the top of her breast. Her skin was smooth and creamy, causing Carmelo's dick to get hard instantly.

"We have a good chance," she told him before the judge came in.

"All rise."

Carmelo quickly stuck his hands in his pants pocket trying to hide his bulge as he stood. Alex argued first. Chris Light was dead and without him they didn't have a case. Maxwell wasn't credible, he snitched for a deal. The prosecutor argued that Chris's statement should still be admissible because of their corroborating statements.

"Yeah, from a paid snitch," Alex cut in.

"Carmelo is a known gang member and could have had something to do with having Chris Light killed," the prosecutor said, causing Alex to stand immediately.

"Your Honor. Mr. Graham has been incarcerated for over three months. He hasn't had one visit; his phones are monitored, and there's absolutely no proof that he's been in contact with any gang members on the phone. There is absolutely no proof, no proof that my client is even in a gang. He's not in a gang book, on a gang file, doesn't have any tattoos, nothing.

"Matter of fact, there are several statements from individuals who say Mr. Graham is not in a gang, so Mr. Giovanni here needs to get his facts straight before he speaks," Alex said, eyeballing the prosecutor.

"Is this true?" the judge asked the prosecutor.

"Is what true?"

"Is what Ms. Perez saying true? Do you have any evidence that Mr. Graham is connected to a gang? That he hasn't had any visits? That there have been no conversations over the phone with any gang members?" the judge questioned.

"Yes, Your Honor. We don't have any evidence that Mr. Graham is in any gang. No, he hasn't had any visits. Yes, the phones are monitored, and we're going through the recordings now, but Your Honor, who's to say that Mr. Graham didn't slip a letter out or a message—"

"I've heard all I needed to hear," the judge said. "I'll take everything into consideration and make a decision. Is there anything else?"

"No, Your Honor," Alex said.

"No, Your Honor."

"Okay, court is dismissed."

# Chapter 74

-------

# Carmelo

Carmelo was used to getting mail. It had been a week since he had gone to court, and although he hadn't told anyone, he was receiving letters asking what happened in court.

He wasn't surprised to see mail on his bunk. He picked the letters up to see who had written to him, and a smile appeared on his face when he saw one from Maria. He hadn't heard anything from her ever since the day at the hospital. She gave birth to his daughter and no one in his family had seen her. She had sent him pictures and they took them. He was reading the letter for the third time when P-Funk tapped him.

"You didn't hear 'em?"

"Huh? What? Hear who?" Carmelo asked.

"The deputy told you to pack up. You're leaving," P-Funk told him.

Carmelo sat there for a minute. "You sure?"

"Nigga, you've been my cellie for two months. I know your last name."

Carmelo went to the door and hit the button.

"Yes," the deputy said into the intercom.

"This is Graham, Carmelo Graham. You told me to pack up?"

"Yes. You're leaving."

"I'm leaving? Where am I going?"

"You're being discharged," the deputy told him. "Roll it up and come to the door."

Carmelo stood there with his head down. He was free. *I'm free!* Carmelo walked to his cell.

"I beat it, my nigga. I'm out of here," he was excited. He shook P-Funk's hand and they hugged.

"Alright, Menace. Take it easy. Don't come back." The fellas were saying as he walked out the door.

Carmelo sat in the holding tank waiting to be released for six hours.

When he finally walked out the door it was after midnight. He inhaled the fresh air and began walking towards Hennepin when he heard a whistle. Carmelo looked back and saw Brian. They shook hands, and Brian handed him a pack of Newports. Carmelo lit one, inhaled, and then exhaled.

"You ready to get this money?" Brian asked.

Carmelo didn't respond, he walked to the car and got in.

# Chapter 75

# Brian

"I don't know if this will fit, but I brought a belt," Brian told him and handed Carmelo a bag.

Carmelo took the clothes out of the bag and began to change.

"Your shoes are in the backseat."

Carmelo put the shoes on and leaned back in the seat. The cigarette had his head spinning. When Brian stopped, Carmelo opened his eyes and looked around, familiar with the neighborhood. Brian opened the glove compartment and handed Carmelo a .9mm and .380.

"Same as before," he said, and Carmelo nodded.

They were robbing the Mexicans again. *This nigga is crazy*, Carmelo thought. Brian looked in the window on the side of the house for a while to see who was in there. When he was satisfied, they walked into the hallway and knocked on the door.

The Mexican who opened the door didn't even ask who it was. Brian pointed a .44 Bulldog at the Mexican's head and ordered him into the house. He said something in Spanish, and when the

Mexican didn't respond, he repeated it again. After a few seconds, Brian looked at Carmelo.

There was a Mexican woman sitting on the couch and Carmelo shot her in the arm. The Mexican put his hands in front of him and yelled in Spanish. Brian repeated his question, and the Mexican led him to another room. Carmelo watched the girl on the couch balled up in pain and wondered if he would give up the drugs and money if it was any of the women in his life. It was a no-brainer for him. He'd give it up if they had a gun pointed at him. Fuck money. A nigga could always get that back, but once a life is gone, there's no coming back.

Brian brought the Mexican into the living room and handed Carmelo the bag. He took a rope from around his waist and tied the Mexican's hands behind his back, leaving the female under a pool of blood.

◆ ◆ ◆ ◆

"You got someplace to go, or do you want to go to the spot?" Brian asked Carmelo.

"Yeah," he said after a minute. "I got someplace to go."

"Where?"

"Maria's."

"She's probably asleep," Brian said and headed that way. "What if she doesn't answer, then what?"

"I'll sleep outside until morning."

They drove in silence. Maria's bedroom window was visible from the street. It was after two in the morning and the light was on.

Carmelo sat in the car for a minute.

"You want me to wait?"

Carmelo grabbed the bag he brought from the county and got out the car.

"Nah, you've done enough." Carmelo closed the door and then ducked his head in the window.

"Thank you," Carmelo said and watched Brian drive off.

# Chapter 76

_____

# Maria

M aria was awake. Chloe had closed her eyes an hour ago and was crying again. Maria wasn't complaining, she loved her daughter, and would stay up all night if she had to. She put Chloe in her arms and sang to her.

"Hush little baby don't say a word . . . Momma's gonna buy you a mockingbird . . . And if that mockingbird won't sing . . . Momma's gonna buy you a diamond ring . . ."

Maria had seen Mel sing to Brian and Brianna and was happy it had the same effect on her daughter. Chloe was asleep, but Maria still held her. She used to love watching Carmelo sleep and seeing her daughter make the same faces made her miss him. She put Chloe in her crib and went into the bedroom. She was about to turn out the light when she heard the doorbell ring.

Maria looked at the clock and saw it was after two in the morning. _Who in the hell is at my door at two in the damn morning_, she thought? She went to answer it because she didn't want whoever it was to keep ringing the bell and wake up Chloe.

Maria turned on the porch light and looked out the door window. She almost fainted when she saw who it was. *It couldn't be . . . It can't . . . He is locked up.* She looked out the window again and saw that Carmelo was still there and unlocked the door.

Maria opened the door and they stared at one another. Carmelo saw the tears running down her face and watched them flow as time stood still.

"Can I come in?"

Maria unlocked the screen door and took a step back. Carmelo walked in and closed the door behind him.

"Can I have a hug?"

Carmelo opened his arms, and she walked into them. Tears ran down his cheeks as he held her.

"When did you get out?"

"An hour or so ago."

"And you came here first?"

"Yes." Carmelo gave her his crooked smile.

"You want to shower?"

"Yes, but first I want to see my daughter."

Carmelo walked over to his daughter's crib and watched her sleep. She was so beautiful, one of his angels. A tear fell down his cheek as he watched her.

Maria took his hand and led him into the bathroom. He watched her as she turned the water on, realizing how great of a woman she was. She sat on the toilet and watched him bathe. When he was done, they went into the room, and he laid down on the bed. Carmelo was asleep before he knew it. He hadn't taken a bath or slept in a soft bed in over three months.

Carmelo woke to the sound of Chloe crying. Maria was sound asleep, with her head on his chest, and her hands in his boxers. Carmelo turned the baby monitor off and went into Chloe's room and picked her up. He sat in the rocking chair and held her. They stared at one another as he talked to her and swore he saw her laugh.

He looked up and saw Maria. Their eyes locked like the first time they met in her backyard. He felt it now, like he felt it then.

"Hey," she said as she walked over to him.

"Hey." Chloe held his index finger.

"You want me to take her?"

"No."

Maria sat on the arm of the chair, and Carmelo put his arm around her waist. She put hers around his shoulders. *A photo moment,* he thought.

"What do you have to do today?"

"Go see everybody else. Carmella expects me to call around noon," he said and looked at the clock. It was 10:38. "If I don't, she's going to go crazy."

"And the rest of them?"

"They're already there. My mom runs a daycare, and my little ones are there."

"You want breakfast?" she asked after a short silence.

"As long as it's food, fried food," he said. "I've eaten donuts and pastries for the past three months for breakfast and I can't eat another one."

Carmelo played with Chloe while Maria made breakfast. When she was done, Carmelo handed Chloe to her and sat down to eat. Chloe began crying immediately.

"She loves me more," Carmelo said with a smile.

"Am I going to see you today?"

"If so, it'll be late. I have a lot to situate, but if you're cool with me coming back late, I will."

"I'm cool."

Carmelo finished eating and went upstairs and got dressed. He called a cab.

"Baby, I could've taken you."

"I'm putting as little stress on you as possible."

"You need money?"

"No, they gave me a hundred in cash, and I have a four-thousand-dollar money order," he told her and watched her facial expression. "There is one thing you can do for me."

"What?"

"Kiss me."

Carmelo leaned down and kissed her. A peck turned into a french kiss, then a passionate tongue wrestle.

"I have to go," he told her when he heard the cab's horn.

"Til tonight," she smiled.

"Til tonight."

Chloe was asleep in Maria's arm, so he kissed her on the forehead and headed for the door.

# Chapter 77

# Carmelo

Tanya had a Kansas City Chiefs Jersey tucked into a pair of tight blue jean pants. She hadn't seen Carmelo since the night he played with her pussy and all she could think about was him. Whenever she was being fucked, she would picture his face and the way he looked at her when he had her on the brink of ecstasy.

She felt bad when she heard that he was locked up. She'd never be able to feel his dick inside of her. She'd never be able to taste his cum. She'd never know what Brandy and Maria felt and why they were so in love with him. When Brian called and told her Carmelo was out, and on his way over, she was wet instantly.

Tanya answered the door and saw Carmelo and Carmella. She stared at him and watched as he checked out her body. When he looked between her legs, she had to cross them. That look, oh, that fuckin' sexy ass look drove her crazy. His smile drove her crazy too. She grabbed the door handle.

"Hey, Carmelo, how are you doing?"

"I'm good," he said as he walked past her.

"Hey, sweetie," Tanya said to Carmella.

"Hey, Tanya."

"You good, my nigga?" Brian asked him.

"Nah, not yet."

"You will be after tonight."

"What time are we leaving?" Carmelo asked, sitting on the couch.

"Around eleven. Why?" Brian asked.

Carmelo put his arm around his daughter's shoulders.

"Because my mini-me is attached to my hip. I told her I was going to let her stay at Tanya's while we were gone and come back to get her, but I think I'm going to take her back to my mom's."

"She'll be asleep before then," Tanya chimed in. "She can stay here, and you can get her in the morning."

"It's up to her," Carmelo said, honestly. "We'll see how she feels in a little while."

Carmella was asleep by ten-thirty.

"I'll be back to get her tonight," Carmelo said, and they left.

# Chapter 78

# Brian

"This is a weight house. The BDs own it. They might have to be forced to give the shit up. You shot ol' girl yesterday. I wanted you to shoot the dude. I hate involving bitches, but it did the trick. Tonight, the same as always, let these niggas know we'll kill 'em, without hesitation, if they don't give us the shit.

When they got to the apartment complex, Brian knocked on the door. As soon as the door was opened, he pointed the gun at the man and put his finger to his lips, silencing him. Carmelo closed the door and locked it.

"Sit down," Brian said in a soft voice.

Carmelo held his pistol on the man as Brian searched the house, returning to the living room with another man.

"Sit the fuck down!" Brian ordered.

*There are supposed to be three of them,* Carmelo thought. *So where is the third one?*

"Whose spot is this?" Brian asked and neither one of them responded. "Since both of y'all know where the shit is, it doesn't

- 212 -

matter which one of y'all I kill. Just know, once you're dead, there's no coming back."

They looked at each other, then the one that came from the backroom spoke.

"This is my house, B," he said, and Carmelo pointed the gun at him.

"Where's the other nigga?" Brian asked. When no one responded, he took a deep breath. "Okay, let's try it this way. Every answer you get wrong or don't answer, your boy gets shot."

Brian stood silent for a minute to let his words sink in.

"You can save yourself, seeing you're the one who might die first," he said and looked at Carmelo. "Arm, chest, stomach, head."

Carmelo nodded his head.

"Where's the third nigga?" Brian asked.

When no one responded, Carmelo shot him in the arm.

"Oh, shit! Fuck!" he yelled and held his arm.

"Next the chest," Brian told Carmelo and turned his attention to the two on the couch. "Where's the third nigga?"

"He went to get the dope," the one who was shot spoke.

"When is he coming back?"

"Within the hour."

"Good," Brian said. "We're getting somewhere. Since you're doing all the talking, I'ma talk to you." Brian looked at Carmelo. "Point the gun at the other nigga, and shoot him in the chest first . . . Now, where's the money?"

The house was silent a few seconds before Carmelo shot the man in the chest.

"Where in the fuck is the money?" Brian demanded. "I'ma give you one last chance, and my nigga's gon kill you. Now, where is the money?"

"In the cabinet," the one shot in the arm said.

The other one was on the floor balled up, bleeding and crying.

"Where? Get up and show me," Brian told him, and they left the room. He returned to the front room in time to hear someone push on the door.

The door opened and a young man in his twenties walked in carrying two duffel bags. Carmelo had his gun pointed at him.

"Drop your bags and put your muthafuckin' hands in the air," Brian commanded.

The young man stood there for a minute, taking in the room. He saw one of his friends on the couch with his clothes drenched in blood and the other on the floor in a puddle of blood. His eyes watered. He looked at Brian, then Carmelo, and dropped the bags. Brian searched him and took the pistol off his waist.

"Go sit the fuck down," he commanded.

Carmelo kept the gun aimed at them, as Brian tied the young man's arms behind his back. Carmelo picked up the two bags and walked out the door with Brian behind him.

# Chapter 79

## C.C.

**"I** talked to Tana and Tiffany last night. They're throwing a Halloween party and want us to come through, A.," Heartless told C.C.

They were on their way to drop some money off to Carmelo's mom.

"That hoe Tiffany is bad as hell too, A.," C.C. replied. "I heard she's a boss freak."

"We'll find out at the party, 'cause I'm trying to fuck somethin'," Heartless said and they laughed.

When the cab stopped in front of the house, C.C. grabbed the bag.

"I'll be back, A.," he said and looked at the cab driver. "Keep the meter running."

C.C. punched in the code that connected him to Carmelo's mom's place.

"Hello?"

"Yeah, this is Cliff, Mrs. Graham," he responded, and she buzzed him in.

He had the whole forty thousand they owed Carmelo and he wanted to give it to his mom.

"Hello Cliff, how are you doing?"

"I'm okay, Mrs. Graham. I just came by to drop off some money for Carmelo," he handed her the bag.

"Oh," she said when she felt its weight. "How much is in here?"

"There's forty thousand in there."

"You want to come in?"

"No, thank you. I have a cab waiting for me outside," he told her. "How is he doing?"

"You want to ask him yourself?" she had a smile on her face.

"Huh?" He was confused.

She opened the door, and he saw Carmelo sitting on the couch next to Carmella. C.C. stared as if he had seen a ghost.

"Who's in the cab?" Carmelo asked.

"Heartless."

"Who?"

"DeWayne."

"Go get him and come up," Carmelo told C.C. and he left.

"What's wrong, A.?" Heartless asked C.C. when he opened the cab's door. "You look like you saw a ghost. Is everything cool?"

"Menace is upstairs."

"What?"

"Pay the taxi and come up, A."

When Heartless saw Menace his mouth dropped.

"How long have you been out for, A?"

"A little over two weeks."

"And you didn't come see us, A?"

"I had to do family time first. Where's Jamal?"

"He's at the pad," C.C. told him.

"Let me get my coat and I'll take y'all home." Carmelo went to get his coat and Carmella got up to get hers.

"Mini-Me, you can't go with me," he said, and she looked at him. "It's not gonna work Mini-Me . . . Daddy will be back to get you. I promise."

# Chapter 80

# Assassins

When they walked into the house, Carmelo saw the lil' niggas who were at his court date. They all got up and shook his hand.

"What's up, A?" Jamal greeted him. "When did you get out?"

"Two weeks ago."

"So, you beat the case A, or you still have to go to trial?" Anthony asked.

"I'm out. I'm good for now."

"That's cool, A," Antonio said, and Carmelo smiled.

"What's up with this A? What does it mean?" Carmelo asked.

We're Assassins," Chad told him.

Carmelo looked at Cliff and DeWayne.

"That's our crew's name. The 187 Assassins," C.C. told him. "Chad's name is Killa C., Anthony is Cain, Antonio is Abel, Jamal is Southside, DeWayne is Heartless, and I'm C.C."

"C.C., huh?" Carmelo said and chuckled.

"Yeah."

"And who am I?"

"You're our O.G. Menace."

Carmelo listened as they let him know everything that went on while he was gone.

"So, the beef died down with them niggas?"

"Yeah A, they've been coppin' pleas ever since," Abel said.

"And what about RedRum?"

"He's cool, A." Southside spoke up. "We all talked. He didn't know the nigga gave us fake fake, plus C.C. gave him twenty-thousand."

"As far as the goods go," Carmelo said after a while, "we're good. Same prices though, until I find a solid connect. Then we'll be alright."

He paused a second and looked at his crew. He didn't know how he'd got here, but he was happy with these lil' niggas.

"How many heats do y'all have?"

"I got three, A," C.C. told him.

"Two," Heartless said.

"Four," Southside told him.

"Me and Abel got five together," Cain said.

"I got six, A," Killa C said and smiled.

"Where you get all those heats from, A?" Southside asked.

"I'm in the streets, A, twenty-four-seven, so I need a lot of heat."

"Killa C is right," Carmelo told them. "Spend the winter trying to get as many heats as y'all can. You can't go to war without 'em."

Carmelo left shortly afterwards.

# Chapter 81

---

# Carmelo

"I need to holler at you," Carmelo told Brian. "It's important." It had been several months, and Brian still hadn't plugged him with a connect. The lil' niggas he had on his team were doing their thang and his dope was getting low.

"I'll be at Tanya's in an hour. Wait for me over there."

Carmelo had seen Tanya a few times over the past few months, and every time she was with a different baller. She'd see him and try to make him jealous, but he'd laugh and see the disappointment in her face.

He walked into Tanya's house and sat down. She tried to act like she was mad and ignored him. That went on for a couple of minutes, and then she walked into the dining room and stood in front of him.

"All right, Carmelo. You win."

"Win what?"

"This pussy's yours."

"So, you're done fucking everybody else?" he said, and she stared in disbelief.

"Huh?"

"I said, if this is mines, that means you're done fucking everybody else."

"You're fucking other bitches," she snapped.

"So what."

"So, you get to fuck other bitches, but I can't fuck nobody else?"

"Yeah."

"Nigga, you got me fucked up. You're cool and shit, but you really got me twisted. I'm not one of these nothing ass bitches you're used to fucking."

Tanya turned around to walk away, but Carmelo touched her thigh and she stopped. He stood and got close to her.

"Tanya, I don't care if we ever fuck, I honestly don't, but I wouldn't mind fuckin' you and fucking with you. I believe we could have some great sex. I believe we can make a lot of money together, too. I don't look at you as a nothing ass bitch. I believe you have a whole lot to offer, but I don't need a gold digger. I've been broke my whole life and I'm not going back to nothing for nobody. Right now, your intentions are to break me, but pussy is not my motivation, money is. Pussy comes a dime a dozen, so if you're not willing to help me get rich, stop wasting my fucking time. Every woman I fuck with will tell you if you ask them, 'I only fuck with Carmelo,' so if you want to fuck or fuck with me, come correct or don't come at all."

When Brian came into the house, they were sitting on the couch watching television.

"What's up?"

"Shit," Tanya told him when he entered the living room.

"What's up, my nigga?"

"Slow motion," Carmelo responded.

"So, what you need to holla at me about?"

"You said when the time came, to holla at you. It's here."

"Time for what?"

"I need a connect."

"How much dope do you have left?"

"Nine bricks."

"That's not enough?"

"For now, but my lil' niggas are going through them, plus what I'm doing. That shit ain't gon' last long, Dog," Carmelo told him. "My nigga, I don't mind jackin'. I don't care about that, but that's here and there. I need a guaranteed hustle. I need guaranteed success."

"So, knowing the brick man guarantees that?"

Carmelo was quiet for a minute. "My nigga, I know what you're thinking, 'Oh, this nigga's young, and if I give him too much, he'll get greedy or fuck up.' My nigga, I've had thirteen kilos of dope at one time and didn't fuck up. I've got nine, but I had seventeen and didn't fuck up. I know I'm not guaranteed forever, but I'm not doing this for me. I don't care about fortune and fame for myself, but I do want it for Mini-Me and the rest of my kids. I do this for them. So, don't think that I'm gonna ever lose sight of that."

Brian looked at Tanya and then back to Carmelo.

"How much do you want to spend?"

"A hundred and fifty thousand."

"Okay," Brian looked at Carmelo. "As soon as you sell the dope you have, I give you my word, I'll hook you up with the connect."

# Chapter 82

———

# Tanya

In April, Brian went to Texas and asked Carmelo to look in on Tanya from time to time.

Carmelo knocked and she opened the door wearing red tights and a white tee.

"What're you doing here?" Tanya asked him.

Carmelo ignored her and walked in. Tanya closed the door and proceeded to walk past him.

"Nuh-uh," he said, and she stopped. It had become their little game. "Come here."

Tanya stood in front of him.

"Closer."

Tanya moved within inches of Carmelo. He touched her face and then kissed her.

"How you doing?" Carmelo asked her.

"Fine."

"I just came to check on you."

"I'm good."

"How's Jamie?"

"She's at school."

"Yeah? So, that means you're here by yourself?"

"Yeah, why?"

"Just making sure. You need anything?"

"No."

"Well, I'm gonna go," Carmelo told her and turned around.

"You don't have to."

"I do. I'll stop by in a few days."

"Why you treat me like this?"

"Give yourself to me."

"I'm trying, and it's driving me crazy."

"Stop trying and do it."

"Will I be able to have friends?"

"Yes."

"Male friends?"

"Yes."

"I just can't get my pussy ate?"

He looked at her, momentarily.

"Come give me a hug. I have to go." He held her.

"I would love to love you. This feels so right. Let's make it right. You and me, nobody else," he whispered in her ear.

"You don't mean it." She stood back and looked at him. "I'll give you all of me. I'll love you unconditionally, but I want all of you."

They stared at each other. "Oh, if it was that simple," he said and kissed her.

She held him tight and then his pager went off. It was Hardtime.

# Chapter 83

---

# Carmelo

Willie James, a.k.a. Hardtime, was another youngster from the hood who had it rough and needed a chance. Carmelo had seen him around for years and decided to give him a shot, like B-Dog had given him.

They'd been booping at the spot on 37th and Cedar the last few months and he liked Hardtime's character. He was fifteen and acted thirty. A young dude from his neighborhood who liked school was something Carmelo had rarely seen. Killa C and Hardtime were eager to make money and wanted to boop thirty days a month, which Carmelo didn't mind. Hardtime went to Folwell Middle School, and Carmelo would meet him at the spot and bring him his goods, protecting him from the possibility of being expelled if he had the drugs with him.

"What's up, A?" Carmelo said to Hardtime.

"I'm at the spot, A, you got me?"

"Yeah, I'm on my way," Carmelo said and got up to leave Tanya's house.

"So, what's up?" Tanya asked.

"I want to lie to you so bad to make you smile, but you know I can't. If I would've met you before I had my kids, I would've given you the world. You would have been my motivation to get rich, my reason for breathing. I'm on a set schedule now. One day I wouldn't mind loving you unconditionally, but I'm not in that kind of position. You ride with me to the top 100 percent, and I promise you, when I make it, I'll put you next to me," he kissed her and left.

Carmelo drove down Lake Street and thought about what Tanya said. He wouldn't mind being with her. She was smart, fine as hell, a hustler, trustworthy, and overall, a good bitch to a certain degree.

Crystal, Maria, Bunny, Jenny, Nena, all of them knew he messed with the other one. His kids were proof of that, yet they all accepted him with open arms. Tanya on the other hand, would be a whole 'nother story. When she's hurt, there's no limit to her revenge. That's why he wanted her to do it his way first, then he'd decide whether or not to make her number one. Carmelo stopped at Clark's Gas Station on Park Avenue to get gas.

# Chapter 84

# Rick G

Rick G sat in jail for two months and did six more in the Workhouse. In his cell at night, he thought about P-Funk and Menace. *Bitch ass muthafuckas gon' jump me over a spades game and some Snickers.* Some nights he got so mad he couldn't sleep. *On Larry Bernard Hoover, if I ever catch either one of them on the block, I'm going to smoke 'em.*

Rick G was at the Park & Lake Car Wash with his cousin Jermaine when he saw Carmelo at Clark's.

"That's one of them niggas who jumped me in the county, G," he said to Jermaine as he watched Carmelo get in his truck and pull off, heading towards Chicago Avenue.

"Where at, folks?"

"In the red Jimmy on gold Daytons going towards Chicago Avenue. Let's go, G."

They followed Carmelo down Lake Street to Cedar Avenue. When he turned on Cedar, Jermaine was a couple cars behind him.

"Slow down, G," Rick G said. "That bitch ass nigga is stopping."

Rick G had the gun in his lap and the window down. Jermaine slowed down as he drove by.

"Bitch ass nigga!" Rick G yelled before he pulled the trigger.

The first shot hit Carmelo in the mouth and went through his cheek. The second shot hit him in the back shoulder, the third in his right arm and the fourth went into his side. The fifth one missed and the sixth bullet hit him in the lower back.

Hardtime ran to Carmelo to make sure he was alive.

"Don't die on me, A," he cried. "Please don't die."

Tears were flowing down his face.

"Take the goods," Menace told him. "Take the goods."

Hardtime took the pouch off Menace's waist.

"Don't die on me, A. I'm here, my nigga," Hardtime slapped Menace when his eyes began to close. "Don't shut your eyes."

"The ambulance is on the way," a fiend told him.

"They're coming A. Stay awake," Hardtime said before he heard sirens.

"Make sure he's not dirty," the fiend told Hardtime. "Check his pockets for dope and shit so they don't send him to jail."

"I already did," Hardtime told him and looked down at Menace. "Keep your eyes open," Hardtime said and slapped Menace again. He reached into Carmelo's pockets and pulled everything out.

The paramedics put Carmelo on the stretcher and rushed to Hennepin County Medical Center.

# Chapter 85

## Carmelo

As Carmelo laid on the ground, he thought about his kids. This had to be the end. He saw pictures of his daughters, Ciara, Colleen, Clarity, Chloe, Carmen, and Carmella.

He thought about his son J.R. He would never be able to play basketball or football with him or see his daughters go to prom. He was tired and closed his eyes. He wanted to rest them for a while, until he felt a slap.

Carmelo opened his eyes and saw Hardtime. He thought about The Assassins. They'll retaliate, there was no question about that, but would they stay together, and become the family they all wanted to each other. B-Dog, his nigga . . . He let his nigga down. Maria, Crystal, Jenny, Bunny, Nena. He was tired, too much was on his mind. He wanted to rest them, but Hardtime slapped him again.

He wouldn't see his little brother graduate, get married, or start a family.

Carmelo saw two white men in white shirts flashing lights in his eyes. *They came to save me*, he thought, and closed his eyes.

# Chapter 86

# The Assassins

The Assassins met Hardtime at the hospital. On the ride over, the only thing C.C. could think about was losing Menace. *What the fuck happened? How did he get caught slipping? Where was Hardtime and why didn't he bust his gun?* He loved Hardtime, they grew up together, even kicked it a few times, *but if he is the reason my nigga dies,* C.C. thought, *he's going in right behind him.*

"What's up? What happened? Where is he?" Heartless asked Hardtime.

"They just took him to the Emergency Room."

The Assassins got off the elevator and rushed the desk.

"Is Carmelo Graham up here?"

"Which room is he in?"

"How's he doing?"

"Is he going to make it?"

"Where is he?"

"Calm down. One at a time," the nurse said. "Are any of you family?"

"Yes. I'm his brother," C.C. told her.

"Call your parents."

C.C. let the tears flow down his cheeks. *Somebody will pay for this*, he thought, as he turned around and walked away, in search of a phone. He had to call Carmelo's mom.

# Chapter 87

---

# Carmella

Carmelo was on life support for three days. The bullet in his side hit a vital organ and the one in his back was close to his spine. Carmelo opened his eyes five days later and saw Maria and Brian sitting in chairs. It seemed as if they were deep in thought. *Could they see me*, Carmelo thought? He wanted to say something, but his mouth was dry, and he couldn't speak.

Carmelo moved his fingers. *Oh*, he felt so weak. He moved them again and Maria looked up. She tapped Brian, then got up and walked to the bed.

"Hey." She had tears in her eyes.

Carmelo tried to speak but couldn't. Brian left and returned with a nurse.

"How are you feeling, Mr. Graham?"

Carmelo's mouth was in pain, so he nodded his head.

Carmelo spent the next six weeks in the hospital going through rehab and physical therapy. He didn't say much during that time. He spent his nights lying on his back, plotting. He would have no more remorse for his enemies. He promised he would never go through this again.

Two times he was caught slipping. There would not be a third. He would condition himself for every situation and get rich in the process.

He was discharged at the end of June. He'd lost over thirty pounds in two months and felt weak. He went from a walker to walking with a cane, to walking on his own. He went to Maria's, thinking Carmella would be waiting for him. He heard she had come to see him when he first arrived at the hospital and hadn't been back since. He asked Maria to take him to his mom's house. Carmella was in her room, the room that had once been his. She glanced at Carmelo when he walked into the room and turned back to the television.

"I know you were scared I was going to die or leave you, but I'm not." Carmelo said as he sat on the bed. "I love you too much to leave you. I've loved you from the first time I saw you standing next to Tiny at the hospital. From that first look until now, I have loved you with all my heart. And when my body leaves you, the love I have for you will never leave. I am going to disappoint you and let you down sometimes; I make mistakes. I'm not perfect, but I don't do them to hurt you. I spend my life trying to make yours better than the one I had. You can be mad at me right now, Mini-Me, but know that I love you more than life. And, when you stop being mad at me, I will be waiting for you with open arms."

Carmelo left the room without looking back. He said goodbye to his parents and opened the door to leave.

"Wait, Daddy!" Carmella said and ran into her daddy's arms crying.

Carmelo cried as he held his daughter.

"I love you, Mini-Me," he told her. "Come on, let's go home."

# Chapter 88

# Tanya

Carmelo got a membership at the YMCA three blocks from Tanya's house. The gym didn't have a shower, so Tanya let him use hers. He'd leave his sweaty clothes and she'd wash them.

She loved him. She knew it the day he was shot. He was like no other man she had ever met. He was young with an old soul, like he'd been here before or something. He had a vision and wouldn't let anybody deter him from it. When she was with him, it seemed like nothing in the world mattered to him except her and she liked that feeling. Plus, he was good to Jamie, but could she give herself to him knowing he wasn't all hers?

The doorbell rang and reality set back in. She went to open the door, already knowing who it was.

"Hey, boy," she said as Carmelo walked through the door.

Jamie was spending the week with her dad, leaving her home alone. She wore a white sundress with a G-string and no bra.

"It's a hot fucking day."

"I know. I damn near passed out at the gym," Carmelo told her as he took off his shirt.

Tanya stared at Carmelo's six-pack as he took his shoes off. *Damn this nigga is sexy*, she thought, as Carmelo headed up the stairs.

"You want some ice water or something?"

"Yeah. I'd appreciate it," he told her, then disappeared into the bathroom.

Carmelo was in the tub when Tanya brought the glass of water to him. He drank some as she grabbed his clothes and turned to leave.

"Tanya!" he called for her. "Have a seat."

She looked at him for a moment before sitting on the toilet. She was sweating.

"How are you doing?"

"Besides being hot?"

"Yeah, besides being hot." He smiled.

"I'm doing okay."

"How's Jamie?"

"Bad as ever. She starts school this year."

"Yeah, Carmella does too," he said, and they sat there in silence for a while, "What you gon' do when she's gone?"

"I don't know. Cook, clean, sleep, something," she chuckled.

"What do you do all day now?"

"Spend time with my daughter or watch TV."

"Now, she's gone and in school, you'll have a lot of free time. Have you ever thought about going back to school?"

"For what?"

"That's a question for you, not me," he told her. "I know you hustle to make ends meet, and I respect that, but you need something that's gonna last. A real job, a steady flow of income, a guarantee.

"I'll tell you what, if you ever decide to go to school, I'll pay for it, free of charge. I don't want nothing back, not even a thank you."

Carmelo grabbed the glass of water and drank it.

"Think about it," he said and started washing his body.

"So, how have you been?" she asked.

"I have my moments, my dreams, my thoughts. That day scared me. I've done some dirty shit to niggas and never thought twice about it, but when the shoe is on the other foot, it's not so pretty.

"I remember laying there. I thought about the people I loved and the things I'd never get a chance to do. I'd never see my daughters go to prom or walk them down the aisle. I'd never get to play basketball with my son or see my little brother graduate. I thought about the people I'd never get a chance to love." He looked at her. "And what might have been . . ."

Tears rolled down Tanya's cheeks.

"Carmelo, I cried when I heard what happened. I thought about you every day and night. I even prayed and I haven't done that ever. I realized when you got shot that I may never get the chance to love you."

She began to cry harder. Carmelo got out of the tub and she stood, putting her arms around his neck. Tanya kissed him and Carmelo pulled away.

"Say it," he looked her in her eyes.

"I'm yours, Carmelo, all yours and nobody else. I love you." She said and kissed him.

Carmelo didn't stop her, instead, he pulled Tanya's dress over her head and took off her panties.

Carmelo lifted Tanya onto the sink and entered her in one motion. She was so wet, so ready.

"Oh, Carmelo," she moaned.

He started a rhythm that her body followed. In and out, up and down. Tanya raised her knees and Carmelo wrapped his arms under them and fucked her. Pumping harder, going deeper, until they came together.

# Chapter 89

# Carmelo

Carmelo drove to Wisconsin the following day to visit his brother Chris. He wanted to see how he was living and conducting himself.

"What's up, A?" Chris asked when he opened the door.

"Shit A, just came to see how you're living up here."

Carmelo walked in and saw his two cousins, Shorty and Smoke.

"What's up, A?" Shorty asked.

"What y'all niggas doing?"

"Chiefing right now. You wanna hit this shit," Smoke asked, extending his hand with the blunt in it.

"Nah A, I'm good. So, what y'all getting into today?"

"Shit, going to a party tonight at this girl's pad."

"That's what's up. What time does it start?"

"Shit, around nine o'clock, but we'll slide through around ten or eleven."

"Cool. I'ma slide with y'all."

"That's cool, A."

In Wisconsin, a party consists of a boombox, beer, and bad dancing. Carmelo watched how his family seemed to be the main attraction. He didn't smoke or drink anymore, and he didn't dance, so he spent his time talking to two White girls named Rebecca and Elizabeth.

Rebecca was an eighteen-year-old blond, slim with nice titties and blue eyes. Elizabeth was a nineteen-year-old redhead with red lips, green eyes, a nice ass, nice titties, and a little weight on her.

When the party died down, they went back to Maniac's place. Elizabeth sat on the couch, while Carmelo and Rebecca went upstairs.

Carmelo closed the door and undressed. He wasn't playing any games. He stood naked in front of Rebecca and let her take in all of him, before putting on a condom. Rebecca took off her clothes and laid in the bed.

*Damn this girl is a freak*, Carmelo thought, as he pumped in and out of her. He'd been fucking the same females for the past few years, adding one here and there, but new pussy was always the best.

He remembered the first time he fucked Tanya in the bathroom, Maria in the bed, Nena at her house, and began getting hard again. He looked over at Rebecca and saw her sound asleep. Carmelo took off the condom, put on his boxers, grabbed another condom, and left the room.

Elizabeth had made herself a pallet on the floor and was under a sheet. Carmelo saw her pants next to her and wondered what she was wearing under the sheet. She opened her eyes and looked at the bulge between his legs. He stood over her and pulled his boxers down. Elizabeth pulled the covers back, inviting him in.

# Chapter 90

---

# Jenny

Jenny worked as a secretary at a big law firm, and went to school three nights a week. She'd been working there a few months when her boss invited her to the firm's Christmas party. She didn't have too many friends and believed she could possibly make some here.

Jenny watched the way her boss was acting and shook her head. She knew the signs. She hadn't sold drugs since she was pregnant, but she knew a fiend when she saw one, and her boss was a fiend.

When he went to his office, he was in such a rush, he forgot to lock the door. Jenny opened the door and caught him snorting a line.

"This isn't what it looks like," he began.

Jenny walked in and closed the door. She walked to his desk, and he looked at the lines of cocaine.

"How much are you paying for that?"

"Huh. What?"

"How much are you paying for that?

"Three thousand an ounce."

"I could get it to you for twenty-three."

Jenny stared at him with confidence. She knew she had him by the balls and waited. It didn't take him long to answer.

"Bring it tomorrow," he told her. "And if I like it, we got a deal."

# Chapter 91

---

# Brad

Brad stood in the circle with his fist ready as three teenage boys surrounded him. He had his mind set to swing until they told him to stop. The first dude hit him on the side of the face, and he staggered to his right. He swung and hit the one closest to him, and his adrenaline began to pump. *Yeah, it's on.*

Brad rushed him and hit him again, this time in the mouth. Then he felt somebody hit him in the back of the head. He turned around and felt a punch to the jaw, then another to his ear. Brad balled up and began to feel punches hit him in his head and his back.

Brad rolled over and felt somebody punch him in his stomach and balled up again. A few seconds later, it was over. Short Dog bent down and helped him up.

"You alright, Lil Blood?" he asked and helped dust Brad off.

"Yeah, I'm bool."

"You're one of us now. You're part of this Brotherhood, this Family. Brotherly Love without Deception, and until you die, it's Blood in Blood out," Short Dog told him and stuck his hand out.

Brad gave him a Blood handshake and they embraced. Brad went around shaking all the Blood's hands, he was a Blood now and it felt good. He just hoped that his cousin Brian felt the same.

# Chapter 92

---

# The Assassins

C.C. loved when it was hot outside. The heat brought more fiends out and more money was made. He had bought a cell phone. He didn't care how big it was or how much it cost, not too many people had them, and if you did, you were balling. Killa C had started curb serving, riding around selling goods, and going off his pager.

Cain and Abel had a spot together, Hardtime and Southside were doing their thang, and he and Heartless were back together.

C.C. walked in the house after copping from Menace.

"I'm glad you're back, A," Heartless told him. "I just ran out of goods."

C.C. handed him the dope and went to use the bathroom. He looked out the window as he was pissing and saw police cars behind the house.

Give me the goods, A," he yelled as he ran out of the bathroom.

Heartless threw C.C. the dope and followed him into the bathroom. He put his gun in the toilet reservoir and C.C. followed.

They were walking down the stairs when the police burst into the house.

# Chapter 93

# Alex

Alex woke up early and sat in the tub, not wanting to go to work. Business had been slow for over half the year and she didn't feel like sitting in an office all day staring at the phone. Her biggest case to date was Carmelo Graham's, and she felt she didn't get the recognition she deserved.

Sometimes she wondered what he was doing. She saw the way he looked at her, with eyes full of lust. *Stop it, girl,* she told herself. *But he's not a kid anymore, he'll be twenty soon.*

She would bend over in front of him, giving him a good look at her round ass. She worked hard on her body five days a week, why not show it off. *What if he would have touched it?* She thought and her nipples got hard. What would she have done? *I wonder if his dick is big?* She ran her hands over her breast, rubbing them across her nipples.

"Ooh," she moaned. *What if these were his hands,* she thought, and then closed her eyes, moving her hand lower.

Alex got out of the tub and dressed. She was walking towards her office when she saw Carmelo, and her heart skipped a beat.

*Tonight*, she told herself, *I'm thinking of Denzel Washington, and I'm going to see if he shows up.*

Alex saw the way Carmelo stared at her, even from a distance she could see him lust. She hoped she wasn't walking funny, because she was nervous. *What did he want? Did he want to ask her out? What will I say? 'I don't date my clients. That was a good one, cliche, but good.*

"Hi, Mr. Graham," she said when she was in earshot.

"So, you remember my name, that's good."

Oh, she forgot about the smile. Alex grabbed her throat.

"What can I do for you?" she found herself asking.

"Can we go inside and talk?"

"Yes, sure," she said and unlocked the door.

Her office was on the second floor and the elevator was down. Alex walked up the stairs slowly. What else could she do, except give him a show?

She didn't have a receptionist, so they walked past the empty desk and she unlocked the door to her office.

There was a desk, a computer, a big shelf filled with law books, and two chairs.

Alex walked behind the desk and sat in one of them.

"So, what can I do for you?" she asked, as Carmelo sat across from her.

"I have two friends in Juvenile I need you to represent."

"When were they arrested?"

"Yesterday evening."

"What for?"

"I don't know. The police raided their house."

"What are their names?" Alex asked as she picked up the phone.

"DeWayne Simpson and Cliff Crawford."

"They're being charged with Possession of a Firearm and Third-Degree sales," Alex said when she hung up.

"Damn. How much time are they looking at?"

"If they get certified, they could get five years alone for the firearm. The possession of drugs depends on how many grams they were caught with."

"How much is it going to cost for you to represent them?" he asked, and she pondered on it.

"Ten thousand for the both of them, twenty if we go to trial."

He picked up the small bag he was carrying and opened it. He pulled out two rubber band stacks and sat it on her desk. She looked at him. *Who is he? His "brother" paid fifty thousand in cash for her to represent him and now Carmelo is giving me ten thousand to represent two juveniles.* Alex counted the money and saw that it was exactly ten thousand dollars.

"What if I would have said twenty thousand dollars to represent them and forty thousand if we went to trial?"

"Then I would have given you whatever you wanted," he said and looked at her with those eyes.

Alex felt her panties get wet.

# Chapter 94

## Carla

Carla moved to St. Cloud the first chance she got. She was tired of the cities and wanted something different. Ever since Carmelo gave her that ten pounds of weed, she hadn't looked back. Her clientele was right, and she was making good money. She was able to move her mom and niece to St. Cloud as well. All her other siblings either stayed in Wisconsin or had their own pad.

Carla wanted to throw a barbecue before Carl went to Illinois for the summer. She had invited everyone except Carmelo but was confident he would come. *It'll be good to have the majority of my daddy's kids together,* she thought.

"What's up, A?" Carmelo asked.

Carla was the only female Assassin. "Shit, I'm throwing a barbecue and want you to come."

"A, I can't. I have my kids and we're going to Valley Fair."

"A, Maniac and em' are coming from Wisconsin, Carl is leaving, Daddy and your mom are coming. We never spend time together as a family, A. Come on, do it for me," she begged.

"Alright," Carmelo said into the phone. "We're coming, knucklehead."

His sister gave him the address and hung up the phone.

◆ ◆ ◆ ◆

Carmelo decided not to wear his bulletproof vest because it was a family get-together. He still packed his pistol, his motto was, 'better to be caught with it than without it.'

He brought Tanya, Carmella, and Jamie with him. When they walked into the backyard, Carmelo watched as all the men stared at Tanya. He knew she was fine as hell and this was the reaction he was going to get. He saw his brother Maniac, and then Rebecca and Elizabeth. *Today is going to be interesting*, he thought. He was there an hour and had to use the bathroom. He was flushing the toilet when he heard a knock on the door.

"Yeah."

"Carla's about to get into it," somebody yelled through the door.

# Chapter 95

---

# Milton

.

Milton was an AAB, and American Aryan Brotherhood member. He had been down in Faribault for the past week. A few of the AABs had gotten into it with some piece of shit Mexicans and the brotherhood sent him and some more guys down there to straighten the wetbacks out.

Milton was watching television and drinking a beer when his eighteen-year-old sister walked into the living room with a black eye.

"What happened to you?"

"I got into a fight with this Black bitch over a parking spot."

"And?"

"She called me a white bitch and told me that she wasn't moving from the parking spot, even though I was there first. I told her to take her Black ass back to the ghetto and her crackhead momma and the bitch punched me in the eye."

"Did you punch the nigger bitch back?" Milton asked.

"No. I couldn't. I fell and she got on top of me and kept punching me."

"Do you know where she stays?"

"Yes. Ebony told me."

"Okay, let's go."

Carmelo walked outside and wondered why his family was bunched up. He walked to the front of the crowd and saw six white guys, and two white females arguing with his family. Carmelo whistled and waited until things were quiet before he spoke.

"Yo, I don't know what's going on, but this is a private party," Carmelo told the white group. "We're not out here to start anything, we're barbecuing and minding our own business."

Carmella and Jamie were there, and he had to protect them.

"What's going on is, that nigger girl right there gave my sister a black eye," Milton said, and everyone began yelling again. Carmelo turned around and looked at his family.

"Shut up!" he yelled at them. "Yo, homie, my sister didn't punch anyone in the face. Maybe you have the wrong group of people."

"Yo, monkey," Milton said to Carmelo, "your bitch ass sister punched my sister in the face and she's going to pay for it."

Carmelo shook his head and took a deep breath, trying to calm himself. "You're not going to touch nobody here. You're going to have to get past me first."

Milton looked back at his crew and then swung. Amateur move. Carmelo was a fighter. He ducked, hit Milton in the ribs twice with his left and then gave him a left hook to the face. Milton staggered and Carmelo began to bounce. Milton rushed him with his head down, and Carmelo sidestepped on him, giving him an uppercut and jab. Milton fell into the alley.

"Y'all grab him and get out of here. We don't want any problems," Carmelo said, and Milton's sister rushed to her brother.

"Come on, Milton, let's go," she pleaded.

Milton moved past his sister and rushed Carmelo. He ducked and scooped Milton, pinning him into the garage, and put his hand around Milton's throat.

"I'm getting mad, you white piece of shit," Carmelo said. "Leave us alone and get the fuck out of here."

He let Milton go and stepped back. Milton walked to his car.

When Carmelo saw Milton open the car door and bend down, he hoped he was reaching for a bat or a chain, but when he saw the pistol, he wished he had never come to the barbecue.

His reflexes were perfect. Without realizing it, Carmelo had his pistol out and was firing it, causing Milton to breakdance as he shot him. When Milton fell, Carmelo walked over to him, and kicked the gun away. He turned around and walked toward the yard.

"Come on," Carmelo told his brother.

# Chapter 96

# Carmelo

Carmelo drove to Eastman Park and threw his gun in the lake.

"Where are we headed?" Chris asked.

"Back to Carla's A, I'm turning myself in."

"Nigga, are you crazy?"

"Nah, I ain't crazy," Carmelo told him. "Why am I going to run when everybody knows I did it? That'll make me look guilty. If I turn myself in, my lawyer can argue self-defense. I have too much going on to throw it all away over this shit."

Carmelo parked a block away from Carla's house. Police tape was preventing cars from entering. He and Chris walked toward the house and were stopped by a police officer.

"Where are you guys going?" he asked.

"My sister lives here," Chris told the officer.

"So what. You can't go in. She's going to have to come out here."

"Well, can you send a detective out here?" Carmelo asked the police officer.

"Why?"

"Because I'm the one you're looking for," he said, and the officer looked at him.

"Carmelo Graham?" the officer asked. "You're the one who shot the man in the alley?"

"No," Carmelo looked the officer in the eye. "I'm the one who wants a lawyer."

Carmelo was handcuffed and taken to the Benton County Jail for PC Manslaughter. It was Friday and he knew Alex wasn't coming to see him until Monday. *Here we go again*, Carmelo thought, as he laid on the hard cot and looked up at the ceiling. He knew he was going to beat the case; he'd done everything right. It was the process he hated dealing with.

Saturday afternoon Alex Perez came to visit him. Her hair was down, and she wore a pink t-shirt that read, 'Got Milk?' with white jogging pants that revealed her camel toe. The room had one chair and she had to stand while they went to get her one.

"So, what happened?"

Carmelo looked her in the eyes, then his eyes drifted down to her camel toe.

"How'd you know I was down here?" he asked, not looking up.

"I saw your face on the news."

Carmelo slowly raised his eyes and stopped at her breast. Her nipples were fat and hard.

"You must have rushed out the house," he said as the deputy brought another chair in. She scooted to the table and crossed her arms over her breast.

"Now that you've had your entertainment, tell me what happened."

Alex took notes as Carmelo talked. She waited until he was done before she responded.

"So, you didn't tell them you did it?"

"No."

"You didn't give a statement either?"

"No."

"That's good."

"So, what's next?"

"They have thirty-six hours to charge you. If they charge you, we go to court; if they don't, then they'll release you."

"So, how much is it going to cost me?"

"Let's see what happens first."

"How much are you going to charge me?"

"Thirty thousand if we don't go to trial, forty if we do."

"I'll have it brought to your office Monday."

"And if you don't get charged?"

"Then it'll be my retainer, seeing that you like being my guardian angel." He smiled and she crossed her legs.

Carmelo was charged Monday morning with 1st and 2nd-degree murder, Reckless Discharge of a Firearm, and Fleeing the Scene of a Crime. The judge set his bail at a million dollars, five hundred with conditions, and a court date was set.

# Chapter 97

---

# Tanya

Tanya reread Carmelo's instructions and made sure she had everything. She met Alex and gave her thirty thousand dollars before heading to a woman named Jenny's house.

Tanya knocked on the door of a huge house in Richfield, Minnesota and waited.

"Who is it?" a woman yelled.

"Carmelo sent me." Tanya answered and the door was opened by a beautiful white woman. "Can I come in?"

Jenny allowed Tanya in and followed her into the day room. Tanya sat the bag she carried on the table and faced her.

"Carmelo told me to give you a quarter and tell you to call the same number when you need more."

Tanya walked past Jenny as smoothly as she walked in, closing the door behind her. There was no need for name changing or small conversations. They weren't friends and it wasn't a social visit.

She paged Southside as soon as she got into the car.

"Who this?"

"Carmelo's woman. He told me to call you. Where can we meet?"

"Who is this?" Southside asked again.

"Menace's woman. He wants me to meet with you."

"I don't know you. I think you got the wrong number," he said and hung up.

Tanya called back.

"What's up?"

"Menace said you were going to be hard to convince. He said to tell you something only him and you would know." Tanya recited Carmelo's message. "He said the day J.J. was killed, you were there and saw who did it. He told you not to say anything to anyone and took you with him to point out the nigga who killed your cousin."

Tanya waited for what seemed like forever. She thought Southside hung the phone up.

"Super America on 35th and Bloomington," he told her.

"Okay."

Tanya drove Menace's Yukon and parked away from the door to the store and the camera in the parking lot. She watched Southside walk to the truck and get in.

"What's up?"

"Menace said to still call his phone. I'm taking care of his business until he comes home."

"Alright," Southside said.

Tanya handed him the bag from the back seat and Southside got out the car. She called Maniac as she drove away.

"This is Tanya, from the barbeque, Menace's woman."

"What's up?"

"Menace said it's all good. I got his phone and pager, so hit me up when you need to," she said and hung up.

Tanya missed this. She hadn't sold dope in years. She'd been a jacker her adult life, and the adrenaline she was now feeling was good. She didn't mind holding her man down while he was locked up, Bonnie and Clyde shit.

# Chapter 98

---

# Carmelo

Carmelo sat in Benton County Jail and waited. The bitch ass prosecutor knew it was self-defense and was trying to book him.

He was there two months before Alex visited with good news.

"Carmelo, how are you doing?" she asked.

"You tell me how I'm doing." He said and she looked offended. "I'm sorry, Alex. These muthafuckas got me so mad. I should have been out this bitch. The punk ass white boy pulled a gun on me first, and his punk ass friends won't tell the truth."

"His sister finally did," Alex told him, and Carmelo smiled. "That's my smile."

"So what now?" he asked.

"The prosecutor called me today and wants to make a deal. Time served if you plead guilty to reckless discharge of a firearm and a year probation."

"I can beat this." It was more a statement than a question.

"The prosecutor is betting that you'd want to leave as soon as possible and not wait another month for trial."

Carmelo sat there and thought about it. They stared at each other and he smiled. "Can we beat this?"

"We can beat the murder charge, but since you don't have a license to carry or even have a gun permit, you'll lose the discharge of a firearm, and they can give you up to five years in prison."

"So, take the deal?"

"I can only present it. It's a good deal. It'll get you out to your kids and family and whatever kind of job that allows you to afford me." She smiled.

"Okay. I'll take the deal," Carmelo told her.

"I'll let the prosecutor know, so she can set a court date, and get you out of here as soon as possible," Alex said and stood. "You have a nice day, Carmelo."

"You too, Alex."

"I'll keep you informed," Alex said and reached for the door handle.

"Alex."

"Yeah," she turned around to face him.

"You should wear your hair down more often. It looks good," he said.

Alex smiled and walked out the door.

# Chapter 99

# Lil B-Dog

Brad a.k.a. Lil B-Dog, wore a red flag everywhere he went. He didn't give a fuck; he was finally a Blood. Twenty-four hours a day, seven days a week, it was Brotherly Love without Deception. He went to Folwell Middle School and was constantly getting into fights with everybody who wasn't a Blood. He went to the parks in the neighborhood questioning every teenager he didn't recognize. Nothing else mattered except representing that B.

When he turned thirteen and realized that being a teenager and a Blood got him pussy, he represented harder. The females at his school and in his neighborhood liked him because he had a reputation. He was a Blood who lived in a Crip neighborhood and seemed fearless.

It was close to the end of the school year and Brad was anxious for summer to begin. It would be his first summer as a Blood and he had to make every day count. His cousin Brian gave him a thousand dollars for clothes, and he knew where to get his attire. Brad asked his sister, Brandy, to drive him to Kaplan Brothers—the only store that sold red Dickies.

When Brad came out of the store, three dudes were hanging around outside and ignored them. He threw his bag of clothes in the back seat and closed the door.

"Yo, Cuz, what you doin' with that dead ass rag on?" one of them asked.

"Yo, Blood, what you doin' with them flew Dickies and flew Chucks on?"

The dude punched Brad in the face, and he returned punches, knocking him down. He knew how to fight and took his stance. Another one rushed him, and Brad hit him twice and then swung on the third dude.

All three teenagers rushed Brad and he started swinging, trying to stay on his feet. Brandy got out of the car and hit one of the teens who punched her in the face, knocking her out. Brad lost his focus and rushed the nigga who hit his sister but didn't make it. He was tackled from behind, slammed to the concrete, and kicked. Brad called Brian when they got home and told him what happened.

"So what do you want to do?" Brian asked him.

"I want to kill them ho-ass niggas."

"I'll be over in a minute."

"Alright, Blood."

Brad was sitting on the couch when Brian walked into the house.

"How's Brandy doing?"

"She's bool. Upstairs laying down," Brad shook his head. "Them bitch ass crab ass niggas knocked my sister out Blood. It's on with them niggas. I know how all three of them look, Blood."

Brian reached in his pocket and pulled out a gun.

"You know how to use it?" he asked Brad, who nodded his head. "You know this is not a game, nigga? Those are real bullets, and they kill, so don't play with that gun. You wanted this life, you got it, so don't cry or complain when you get jumped or in a fight. A real Blood rides for his crown."

Brian handed Brad the gun.

"Thanks, Blood."

"You know if you ever get locked up what to say?"

"What?"

"What the fuck you mean 'What?' What do you say if the police ask to talk to you?"

"I say no."

"You say, 'No, I want a lawyer.'"

"Okay."

"No, not okay, you say, 'I want a lawyer.'" Brian told him. "Now I want to hear you say it."

"I want a lawyer." Brad said and Brian stood to leave.

"Call me if you ever use that," he said and walked out the door.

A month later Carmelo's cell phone rang. It was Tanya.

"What's up?"

"Where you at?"

"I'm at the stoplight on Lake and Chicago. Why?"

"Come to my grandma's."

"What's up?"

"Brad shot somebody, and Brian's gone."

Carmelo was with C.C. and Heartless. The three of them had their pistols out and ready when they pulled in front of the house on 26th and Bloomington. It was in the middle of the Crip neighborhood and Carmelo wondered how Brian or Brad made it living there.

Tanya, Brandy, and Brad were on the couch when they walked into the house. Tanya ran to Carmelo and hugged him.

"What happened?" he asked Brad.

"I went to the corner store on 28th and some older niggas started set trippin', so I started set trippin' back. The grown nigga spit in my face and punched me. The other nigga took my flag out my pocket, lit it on fire, and walked away laughing. I got up, pulled my gun out, and started shooting."

"Where's the gun?" Carmelo asked and Brad handed it to him.

"Give me your keys," he told Tanya.

"A, you and Heartless go get rid of this." He handed the gun and keys to C.C.

"Why did you go to the corner store? Super America is a block away?" Carmelo questioned Brad.

"I don't know."

"How fucking dumb are you? Do you want a name that bad? You stay right here idiot, and these niggas know where you live. Your grandma stays here, your sister, my daughter comes here to visit. You don't fuckin think about shit, do you?

"What if these niggas shoot up the house and hit your granny or my daughter? Then what? Now I have to kill them and you for doing this dumb ass shit." Carmelo was furious. "If they send the police here you better not say shit. Ask for your lawyer and keep your fuckin mouth closed."

"The police are gone from down the street," C.C. said as he and Heartless walked into the house.

"When is Brian coming back?" Carmelo asked Tanya.

"Next week."

"Give Tanya back her keys, A." Carmelo told C.C. before turning his attention to Tanya. "Go grab me some clothes to last me until Brian gets back."

"Yo, A, you stayin' here?" C.C. asked.

"Yeah."

"Well, we ain't going nowhere."

"A, I need y'all to take my car to my pop's pad then."

"Yo, A," Heartless cut in. "Have Tanya follow you to drop your car off, then y'all go get some clothes and come back. We'll stay here."

Carmelo put his car in Bunny's garage and grabbed the bag of guns he had stashed. They drove to Tanya's house next.

"What are you doing?" Carmelo asked when he saw her putting her clothes in a suitcase.

"I'm staying too."

"No, you're not."

"Baby, that is my grandmother's house. Those are my cousins. I am staying."

"Who's going to watch Carmella and Jamie for the next five days?" Carmelo asked her.

"Your mom can. They're in school until four, so she only has to feed them dinner, bathe them, and put them to bed."

He knew he couldn't win. "Okay."

"This is how we'll do it, A." Carmelo told C.C. and Heartless when he was back at the house. "Y'all take the night shift, send Killa C and the twins through in the mornings and y'all switch off."

Carmelo hadn't said one word to Brandy since the day at the hospital and seeing her now made him mad. She came to him while he was in the kitchen.

"Can I talk to you, Carmelo?"

"No," he told her and walked past her.

# Chapter 100

# Brian

Brian walked through the door of his grandmother's house and couldn't believe his eyes. Tanya, Carmelo, and Killa C were on the couch watching television, the twins sat by the front window, and Brandy and Brad were in the dining room.

When he'd gotten back to Minnesota, he called Tanya and she told him everyone was at his grandmother's, but hadn't told him why. He was worried something had happened to his grandmother, until he saw Carmelo and his crew.

"What the fuck is going on?" He asked no one in particular.

"Go ask your gang bangin' ass cousin." Carmelo told him.

Brian stood speechless as Brad told him what happened. *How fuckin' dumb is he?* Brian thought. *I should have never allowed him to become a Blood. He's not ready for this way of life and this shit right here proved it. Now I have to lace up my Chucks again.*

Brian looked at Menace and felt real love for him. The lil nigga stayed at his grandmas for five days. It got no more real than that.

Brian called Carmelo into the kitchen.

"Good looking out, my nigga."

"What you wanna do?" Carmelo asked. "The niggas ain't tried shit, but you never know. You wanna wait to see what they do, or you wanna bring it to 'em? My niggas are ready and I'm ready, but it's your call. What's up?"

Brian thought about it. If he started a war with these niggas, there would be no stopping, no foul plays, no techs. Everybody would be fair game, including his grandma, Brandy, Melinda and his kids, and no telling who else. He'd have to move his family from this neighborhood before he made any move.

"Nah, it's all good." Brian told him. "I'm going to stay here until I come up with a plan."

"Alright, Bro. Call me anytime, you know I'm coming."

"I will." Brad and Carmelo embraced. "Love, Bro. I appreciate this. You're a real nigga."

"You're my big brother. It comes with the love."

# Chapter 101

—————

# Carmelo

Carmelo was at the stoplight on 38th when he saw P-Funk at Portland Foods.

He pulled into the parking lot and they embraced.

"What's up, my nigga?" Carmelo said.

"Shit, what's good?"

"When did you get out?"

"A few weeks ago. I bee you're out here getting it. Driving in the flame Old School on hundred spokes, and you're wearing Polo from head to toe?"

"I'm living day to day, my nigga. What you on?"

"I'm about to go to the spot with my brother. We're trying to get this money before we head back to Barson Bity."

"Out West?"

"Yeah, my Nigga. I ain't been there in over two years."

"That's cool, my nigga."

"You should bome out there with me, Dog. You'll love the Pad."

"I'll think about it. I remember how you used to talk about it when we were cellies."

"Have you caught Rick G?" P-Funk asked Carmelo.

Carmelo shook his head at how stupid people were. He didn't know who shot him in front of Hardtime's spot. He had taken it as a lesson, he was slipping and couldn't be mad, only conscious.

He found out when he was released from the hospital that one of the Blood girls overheard a conversation Rick G had bragging about shooting him, and she told Bunny. *Why niggas talk about the dirt they did was beyond him*, Carmelo thought. He hadn't seen Rick G, but when he did . . .

"Nah, I haven't."

"Punk ass nigga."

"Let me get your number, my nigga,"

"You be bareful." P-Funk said as he handed Carmelo the piece of paper.

The two men shook hands and Carmelo walked to his car.

# Chapter 102

# Carmelo

Carmelo parked in front of Maniac's house and wondered how his family members could live around all these white people and be comfortable? How could they tell who was the police and who wasn't?

"What's up, A?" Carmelo asked when Maniac opened the door.

"Shit. What's good, A?"

"Kicked back, waiting on you."

"I'm here. Let's go to the room."

Carmelo gave Maniac the dope and watched as his brother went into the closet and grabbed a shoebox.

"Yo, A, do you keep your goods and money here?"

"Yeah," Maniac answered nonchalantly.

"Stop doing that. I told you before, I've seen so many niggas jacked because they keep all their shit in one place. Then what? What you gon' do? Go from a key to a quad?"

"Come on, split your money between bitches or hide it at your mom's pad. Get your own place in Minneapolis to hide your money and sell your goods up here. You're playing a dangerous game, A. It's even deadlier because you're letting Marie know all your business. My nigga, I love you A, you're a reflection of me, you're a part of me A, and you're putting me in jeopardy by letting her know I supply you. My nigga, start being smart, A. Start being smart," Carmelo said and left the room.

When he got to the bottom of the stairs, he saw Rebecca and Elizabeth sitting on the couch. He liked the girls for their loyalty. They stayed in contact with him while he was in the county and did what they could. This was the first time they'd seen one another since he'd been released.

"What's up?" Carmelo said and smiled. "Quit staring and come give me a hug. How have y'all been?"

"Fine," Elizabeth responded and kept her arm around his waist.

"What y'all doing over here?"

"They're always over here. They ain't got no life," Maniac told his brother.

"What are y'all doing tonight?" Carmelo asked.

"Nothing," Rebecca said.

"Are you staying here for a while?" Elizabeth asked and Carmelo smiled.

"Are we going to do what I wrote in the letter?" he asked.

Carmelo wanted to have a threesome.

Elizabeth giggled. "Ask Rebecca."

"No, you ask Rebecca," Carmelo said and turned to his brother. "I'm gone A, call me. Bye Marie."

He walked toward the door.

"Carmelo," Rebecca called out and he stopped.

"What's up?"

"Yeah."

"Yeah what?"

"Yeah, we'll do it," Rebecca said and smiled.

"Let's go," he said, and they followed him out the door.

# Chapter 103

# Brian

B rian sat in his grandmother's house and watched television with his kids. He hadn't been home in two weeks and they wanted to spend time with him.

He looked at his kids and thought about his life. He had a wife that loved him, money, beautiful kids, a nice family, and a good friend, a real friend. What more could one ask for?

*It's crazy,* Brian thought, *Carmelo has a baby with my younger cousin, one by my sister-in-law, and is fucking my first cousin, Tanya.* Brian wasn't mad at him, because as weird as it sounded, he knew Carmelo was a good nigga, and would provide for them all.

He heard Melinda's horn.

"Your mom's outside. Let's go."

Lil Brian and Brianna gathered their things and the three of them walked to the car.

"I love you," he told his son.

"I love you too, Dad."

"You take care of your mom and sister. I'll be home in a few more days."

"Okay," his son said as he got into the front seat.

"I love you too," Brian told Brianna and hugged her.

"I love you, Dad. Can we come back tomorrow?"

"Of course." He smiled and closed the door when she got into the car.

Melinda was standing outside the car when he made his way to her.

"I miss you."

"I miss you too, Baby," he told her. "I'll be home in a few more days. Things are quiet and ain't nobody tried shit. I'm going to stay until Sunday night, and I'll be home for good."

"I can't wait," Melinda said and hugged him. "I love you."

"I love you more."

Brian watched as they drove away.

# Chapter 104

# Carmelo

Carmelo looked in the mirror and smiled. He was a mutha fuckin G. He had two bitches in the bed naked.

"You did your thing," he said, looking at his dick. "I'm proud of you."

He walked to the dresser and picked up his pager to see what time it was. 6:33 p.m.

Carmelo watched as Elizabeth walked to the bathroom. *She looked good naked.*

"Come here." He told her when she came back into the room.

"What?"

"You ready for round two?" he asked her.

Elizabeth grabbed his dick and licked her lips while Rebecca laid on her back with her legs open.

Carmelo was ready for round two and was heading for the bed when his phone rang.

"Yeah."

"What's up, my nigga?"

"How you are doing, Dog?"

"I'm good, Mel just came and got the kids. I was thinking about you. I ain't seen you in a while."

"Nigga, I was just there three days ago."

"Yeah, I'm just fuckin' with you," Brian said. "I've been over here thinking about a lot of shit."

"Like what?" Carmelo sat on the edge of the bed.

"Life . . . everything. My lil relative is already following in my footsteps, and I ain't trying to see him locked up or dead. He ain't never have a mom or dad and I know he looks up to me. I think, no, I know I'm dropping my flag, and I'm going to make him drop his. I'll start spending more time with him and show him something different. I have enough money and time to raise him and give him everything he needs. Do him like you do Carl."

"That's real."

"I'm glad we met. I watch you and I see how you're willing to sacrifice yourself for those you love, and I respect that. I'm glad I got to be a part of that."

"Dog, you're the realest nigga I know, my real brother, and I love you for what you did for me. I'll be forever grateful, because without you I wouldn't be shit. That's real talk, my nigga. It's cool what you're doing for Brad and for yourself. If you need me, let me know and I'll help you in any way I can," Carmelo told him, and they were quiet for a while.

"We sound like old women," Brian said, and they laughed.

"Nah, we sound like good friends."

"What you doing tonight?"

"Why, what's up?"

"You wanna go to the bar and shoot some pool?"

"Yeah, we can. I'll be back by ten. I'm leaving Wisconsin in a minute."

"Alright. One." Brian said and they hung up.

Carmelo watched Elizabeth and Rebecca laying naked on top of the covers and felt his dick getting hard.

"One more before I go," he said and walked toward the bed.

# Chapter 105

## Casper

Casper sat in the car and watched the slob nigga's house. The lil nigga thought he could stay around the Locs, represent that slob shit, and shot two of his homies? Fuck nah. Every night since then he'd been sitting down the street waiting to catch the lil nigga, with no luck. It had been two weeks and he was about to give up the stakeouts when he saw the older slob nigga he knew from back in the day. The nigga didn't gangbang, but he was still a slob and being associated sometimes could make you a casualty of war.

Casper crept through the back and stood on the side of the house. He heard the nigga hang up the phone and watched him stare at the street. Casper walked from the side of the house and looked the nigga in the face before he pulled the trigger, emptying his clip.

# Chapter 106

## Carmelo

Carmelo dropped Elizabeth and Rebecca off and stopped to get gas. He was getting on the highway when his phone rang.

"Yeah," he answered.

"He's dead," Tanya said into the phone and Carmelo pulled over.

"What you say?"

"He's dead!" Tanya cried and Carmelo's stomach dropped.

"Who's dead?" he demanded.

"Brian!" she was crying hysterically.

"He's not dead. I just talked to him." Carmelo couldn't believe what he was hearing. He just talked to Brian less than two hours ago. "Baby, where are you?"

"I'm at my grandma's."

"Where's Dog?"

"He's lying on my grandma's step," she told him, and his stomach dropped.

"Baby, I'm on my way. I'll be there as soon as possible. Where's Jamie and Carmella?"

"In the house."

"Okay, go be with them. I'll be there in a minute, alright?" he said and hung up.

So many thoughts were going through his head. He was planning on telling Brian about his first threesome. Now, he realized it was the threesome that probably got him killed. Carmelo usually drove to Wisconsin, got his money, and came back to Minneapolis. Today, he stayed to get some pussy, and now his friend was dead.

How were Mel and the kids doing? Carmelo called Maria.

"Hello?" she answered on the first ring.

"How are you doing?"

"Not good, Carmelo. Brian's dead," she was crying.

"How's Mel and the kids?" he asked, and she began crying hysterically.

"I'll be there soon," Carmelo said and hung up the phone.

He couldn't take too much right now. Hearing everybody in pain and not being able to fix it brought a sense of rage and helplessness over him.

Carmelo parked two blocks away and walked through the crowd. The Assassins were standing amongst them.

"What's up, A?" C.C. said when he saw him.

Carmelo looked across the street at Brian's body, which had not been covered. His legs and waist were on the porch stairs while the rest of his body laid on the porch. Half his face was gone, and Carmelo felt the tears begin to roll down his cheeks.

Brian had so many plans, so many dreams and ideas. He wanted to get them to a place where there was no more jacking or dope selling. No more guns and looking over their shoulders. He didn't know how, but he saw better days, and now somebody killed his friend, his brother.

Carmelo wiped his face and called Tanya, who told him to come through the back.

When he walked through the door she ran into his arms and cried.

"He's gone, Carmelo!" she cried. "Brian's gone."

# Chapter 107

# Detective Turner

A short time later, Detectives Turner and Young walked through the door.

"We just came to tell you that the coroner is here and is going to be moving Mr. William's body soon. We'll call you within the next few days about his property." Detective Turner told Brian's grandmother.

He looked into the kitchen and saw a few teenagers that weren't there earlier and decided to see who they were. Detective Turner stopped dead in his tracks when he saw Carmelo sitting at the table with Cliff and DeWayne standing behind him.

"Hi, Sir. I'm Detective James Turner," he said to one of the teens and extended his hand. "What's your name?"

"Lawyer," the teen told him.

Detective Turner looked at Carmelo. "See you soon."

*This case just got interesting*, Detective Turner thought as he walked away. The homicide victim was connected to Carmelo, a known murderer. Cliff and DeWayne are here too, also known murderers. The other five, if they hadn't killed, they would. Yeah, this was about to get ugly.

"Your schedule full?" Detective Turner asked his partner.

"I'm coaching my son's Little League Softball team this summer."

"Clear it, we're in for a long summer," Detective Turner said and filled his partner in on what he had just witnessed.

# Chapter 108

# Carmelo

The night before Brian's funeral, Carmelo went to the apartment in Northeast. The first place Brian ever brought him. They shared so many memories there.

Brian was a lively person. Every time he walked in this house; Brian was eating something. Carmelo didn't understand how Brian wasn't a fat nigga, when all he did was eat. They had some of the realest conversations in this place.

Carmelo sat on the couch and cried. Tomorrow was the last day he'd see Brian before he was buried for good. Carmelo knew what he had to do. There was no doubt, no question, and there'd be no regrets. He only wanted to make sure his kids were taken care of. He grabbed a pen and a piece of paper to make preparations. After he finished, he went into his room and grabbed the black duffel bag on the floor.

◆ ◆ ◆ ◆

Carmelo woke early the next morning, showered and dressed. He called Tanya as he walked out the door.

"Hello."

"Hey, baby, it's me. How you doing?"

"I miss him, Carmelo." She sounded so sad, and his heart ached for her.

"I do too, Baby."

"Where are you?"

"I have something I have to do."

"You know the funeral starts in an hour?"

"I'll be there, I promise. I need you to do something."

"What?'

"Get a video camera and film the funeral."

"What? Why?" she asked him, confused.

"Could you do it? Grab the one in the room and record the funeral. I'll be there as soon as I can."

"Baby, what are you doing?" she asked him with fear in her voice.

"I need you to do that for me. Can you do that for me?"

"Yeah."

"Okay, I'll see you in a little while. I love you."

"I love you." He said and hung up.

Carmelo walked into the funeral just before it was time for him to speak. He had just left Webb's Barber Shop, and as he walked to the podium, he felt everybody staring at him. He looked at Brian in the casket before he spoke.

"If you were looking for a friend, he was one. If you were looking for a father figure, you had one in him. If you were looking to see how to treat your wife, you could watch him. If you were looking for advice, you could listen to him. If you were looking in the dictionary for a picture of love, you'd see his face.

"I talked to Dog before he died and he told me he was giving up his life, his old friends, and everything that wasn't positive for his cousin. He didn't want his cousin to have the same life he had.

He wanted something better for Brad. That's love. He was willing to give up, no, he gave his life for his cousin. He died protecting his family, that's love. Now he'll never be able to see his kids grow up. He'll never see his son score the winning basket or get his high school diploma. He'll never see his daughter's prom dress or walk her down the aisle. He'll never be able to grow old with his wife and sit side by side in the park and watch his grandkids run and play."

Carmelo had tears running down his face. He looked down and spoke again.

"He took me in when I had nothing. I didn't have a dollar to my name or a piece of gum in my pocket. All I had was three females pregnant with no way of taking care of the kids inside of them. He saw my fear, my pain, and my sincerity. He saw my heart and he helped me when no one else did. Not my family, not my homies, nobody. He was a real friend, a true brother. They took the wrong one. These niggas took the wrong one."

Carmelo let the tears run and didn't speak for a minute.

"He'll be missed. He will be remembered. He will be loved . . . They killed the wrong one," Carmelo said and stepped down.

At the reception, Carmelo saw people from the neighborhood he hadn't seen since an adolescent. *These niggas didn't love B-Dog.* He saw Johnny B and they shook hands.

"What's up, Menace? I like what you said."

"Thanks."

"It'll be different with him gone."

"I know."

"Yo, you're a real nigga, if you need me for anything you know where to find me. B-Dog trusted you, so I trust you."

"Good looking."

Carmelo saw J-Moe and knew he had to get things situated. He didn't see Tanya and decided to talk to him on his own.

"What's up, Menace?"

"Not too much. How you doing, J-Moe?"

"You know me and Brian go back to elementary, so I'ma miss my nigga."

"I need to holler at you." Carmelo told him and they walked to a corner.

"What's up?"

"The prices stay the same?" Carmelo asked.

"Yeah, the prices stay the same."

"Good, I have four hundred thousand dollars."

"Whoa, slow down. Give me two hundred thousand and I'll give you twenty-five birds. Hold on to the other two."

"I may be leaving soon, but I'm going to have you doing business with a woman I trust," Carmelo told him.

"Who is she?" J-Moe asked as Tanya walked up.

"Hi, Jamie," Tanya greeted J-Moe.

"Hi, Tanya."

"So y'all know each other already?" Carmelo said, feeling better about his decision already.

"Yeah," J-Moe said. "Since grade school."

"Okay, that's cool then. This is who I was talking about. She's going to be dealing with you for a while."

"Cool," J-Moe said, looking at Tanya.

"I'ma give her your number so she can get at you when she needs to," Carmelo told him.

"She already has it," he said, and Carmelo gave him a strange look.

"Daddy!" Jamie said and ran into J-Moe's arms.

Carmelo looked from J-Moe to Tanya, smiled, and then walked away.

# Chapter 109

# Carmelo

"Get everybody and meet me at the spot," Carmelo told C.C. and left.

*So J-Moe is Jamie's dad?* Carmelo had mixed feelings about the whole situation. He wanted to be mad at Tanya for not telling him but couldn't be. As far as he knew, no one said anything to anyone. On the flipside of things, J-Moe wouldn't cheat Tanya. He'd try to fuck, but who wouldn't. Right now, he had a truck full of guns and needed to get them to a safe place.

"So we're going to war, A?" Killa C asked when Carmelo sat the bag of guns on the floor.

"Yeah, but not yet."

"What are these for?" Cain asked.

"I'm just relocating some heat for easier access, A."

"So what's the plan?" C.C. asked.

"We'll wait 'til the middle of next month, then we'll start smokin these niggas." Carmelo told them. "Give y'all time to stack y'all dough, A."

"I'm ready now, A. We can kill all them bitch ass niggas," Abel told him.

"It's not time, A. Too many people are watching, plus them niggas are probably hiding. We want them to be sitting ducks waiting to be picked off." Carmelo told the Assassins. "If anything happens to me, whether I die or go to jail, listen to C.C., then Heartless, and then Southside. As far as goods, I have the same female booping for me and y'all have her number. Don't give it to anyone, not even Maniac, he's letting his bitch know and see too much. He's still an A, but I'm not going to let his stupidity jeopardize us all."

Carmelo got up to leave.

"We got you, A?" Heartless told him.

"I know y'all do." Carmelo smiled. "C.C., let me holla at you."

C.C. followed Carmelo outside.

"Yo, A, I need a stolen G-ride by next week. Put it in Beatrice's garage and don't let her see you do it."

C.C. was fuckin Bunny's little sister.

# Chapter 110

----

# Carmelo & C.C.

Three weeks later, Carmelo looked at the clothes he laid out on the bed. You know a person loves you when they are willing to sacrifice their life for you. At that moment, Carmelo thought about Mel and the kids, how empty they were now without Brian. He was their protector. Brian took care of his grandma, making sure she had everything she needed financially, from medication to food. He was also a true cousin to Tanya. Carmelo didn't know the situation between J-Moe and Tanya and why Tanya had to jack niggas, when J-Moe had all the money. Brian didn't throw that in Tanya's face, instead, he helped her get to where she was. Brian was a great older relative to Brad. He was willing to change his entire life to save him.

A tear fell down Carmelo's cheek. *And these bitch ass niggas killed him.*

Carmelo put on a black Dickie t-shirt, blue Dickie pants, and black Nike shoes. He wore his vest and carried a Smith and Wesson .9mm with an extended magazine and hollow points on his waist.

Carmelo called C.C. "You ready, A?"

"Yeah."

"I'll be at the garage in twenty minutes."

"I'll be there, A." C.C. said and hung up the phone.

C.C. stood outside the garage while Carmelo put the .223 Fully Automatic Assault Rifle in the backseat of the stolen car. He took a wig with long braids out of a bag and put it on his head.

"Let's go, A." He said and got into the passenger seat.

C.C. got into the car and pulled off.

They drove in silence. They were on a mission and it was time to reflect and think, not talk.

C.C. drove through the Crip neighborhood and on Franklin Avenue looking for anybody, but there wasn't anyone in sight.

Carmelo was getting discouraged and was going to tell C.C. to take him back to his car when they turned on 12th Avenue.

Carmelo smiled when he saw Steward Park filled with blue Dickies and blue bandanas.

C.C. drove past and Carmelo watched as three dudes jumped on one. *Oh*, Carmelo thought, *this is a gang meeting.*

C.C. drove to the end of the block and parked on the corner closest to where the Crips stood. Carmelo calmly got out of the car and opened the back door. He reached in slowly, grabbed the Assault Rifle, turned around, aimed and fired.

Only when the tension was gone from his arm and Carmelo heard the click, did he turn around and throw the Assault Rifle in the backseat. He quickly got into the car and C.C. sped down 12th Avenue, slowing down as he crossed Lake Street.

Carmelo got out of the car at Bunny's and walked into the garage, took off his wig, and hid the .223 as C.C. drove off. Carmelo picked C.C. up on 44th and 2nd a few minutes later and they headed toward the pad. They needed to talk.

# Chapter 111

# Casper

C asper woke up feeling good. Today was the day he became a Six-0 Crip. He loved his niggas from Bogus, but they weren't on shit. The Locs was always on something and ran shit. Them niggas got money, showed unity, and had each other's back. Plus, the Crips were everywhere, not just South Minneapolis, like Bogus. He'd have an army behind him now. *Crip or Cry, Do or Die.* Casper got out of bed and showered. The meeting started at one and he had to get ready.

Casper stood at the bottom of the hill and looked around. *Damn, there were a lot of Locs here,* he thought, some he had never seen before. He was being C-ed in with four other niggas and wanted to go first. Sixty seconds later it was over, and Casper was a Rollin Sixty's Crip. The hugs and handshakes came next, then another homie got in the circle.

Casper was wiping his eyes when he saw the car drive past. He could see a light-skinned nigga driving, but his vision was blurry. He watched as the car drove up the block and stopped. *It was probably some of the homies showing up late*, he thought, and was about to turn around when he saw the nigga getting out of the car.

*That looks like Menace*, he thought, but saw the blue Dickies. Casper looked down at his shirt and saw blood on it. *Fuck, I have to go home and change.*

Casper looked up just in time to see the nigga aim the rifle and begin shooting. He fell to the ground.

# Chapter 112

## Detective Turner

D etective Turner and Detective Young sat at their desk bored. Detective Young wanted to coach his son's Little League Softball team this summer, instead, he handed it to another kid's father because he had to work. He saw the look of disappointment in his son's eye and heard it from his wife. And for what, a false alarm?

"I'm going to my son's softball game. If anything happens, don't call me." He said sarcastically and put on his blazer.

"I'm coming too," Detective Turner said as he got out of his chair. "I gave Carmelo too much credit."

"Yeah, you did," Detective Young said as they walked out the door.

◆ ◆ ◆ ◆

Detective Young stood next to his wife and watched as his son hit a home run. Detective Turner thought it was going to be a boring game and only came because it beat being behind the desk.

It was the bottom of the sixth when his pager vibrated. Their two-way radios were in the car and Detective Turner went to use the phone in the vehicle.

He ran to where his partner was. "Gotta go." He was out of breath.

"Why? What happened?" Detective Young asked.

"That son of a bitch shot up a park."

Detective Young kissed his wife.

"Thank you for showing up." She told him.

"I'm happy I came. I'll see you later."

"Be careful. I love you."

"I will. I love you, too."

# Chapter 113

## Casper

Casper got off the ground and looked at his homies. He had never seen no shit like this before. One of his homies laid next to him with half of his face gone. Tears rolled down his cheeks and shit ran down his legs at the same time. *That nigga Menace was muthafuckin' crazy.*

Casper saw several niggas laying down scattered across the park. Another homie was shot in the stomach and his intestines were everywhere. He stared at Casper with tears running down the sides of his face, taking short breaths. His hand was outstretched, and Casper wanted to take it, to show some kind of aid and assistance, but he couldn't move. Casper watched as he took his last breath, and instead of being mad or sad, he was scared. *That could have been me,* he thought, and began to cry.

# Chapter 114

---

# Carmelo & C.C.

Carmelo and C.C. sat at the house and talked. He had showered and burned the wig in the tub.

"I'm gonna need you to use that rifle again before you get rid of it." Carmelo told C.C. "I'll let you know when."

"Alright."

"I'm leaving you in charge. This is not a gang, A. We're getting money to support our family, to help each other. Leave the gang bangin to them niggas who ain't got shit to lose."

"All right, A."

"You're a real nigga. I love you, A. Take care of yourself and your brothers."

"I love you Menace. Be careful, A," C.C. said, and then they shook hands. Carmelo called P-Funk.

"Yeah, who this?"

"It's Menace."

"What's up, my Nigga?"

"Shit. You still goin' out West?"

"Yeah, we're about to mash in about an hour."

"You got room for me?"

"You wanna bome?"

"Yeah, my nigga."

"Yeah, we got room. Bome to my pad."

Menace hung up, grabbed his fake ID, ten grand, and walked out the door.

He was headed to Cali . . .

# END OF BOOK ONE